U0079317

I am English
Conversation King

我是英語
會話王

國家圖書館出版品預行編目資料

我是英語會話王 / 王愛實著. -- 初版.
-- 新北市: 雅典文化事業有限公司, 民112.05
面; 公分. -- (全民學英文; 68)
ISBN 978-626-7245-11-8(平裝)
1.CST: 英語 2.CST: 會話
805.188   112002243

全民學英文系列 68

我是英語會話王

作者／王愛實
責編／張文娟
美術編輯／姚恩涵
封面設計／林鈺恆

法律顧問：方圓法律事務所／涂成樞律師

總經銷：永續圖書有限公司
永續圖書線上購物網
www.foreverbooks.com.tw

雲端回函卡

出版日／2023年05月

雅典文化

出版社
22103　新北市汐止區大同路三段194號9樓之1
　　　　TEL　(02) 8647-3663
　　　　FAX　(02) 8647-3660

前言

　　想知道外國人在日常生活中真正使用的英語嗎？

　　英語唸得很多，遇到外國人雖然可以溝通，可是想要就像母語人士一般順暢表達、完全聽懂，這時就需要多接觸，多練習了！

　　本書讓您彷彿置身在英美語系國家，帶領您進入母語人士在各種場合中的對話!

　　從家裡、煮菜、餐廳點餐、購物中心、百貨公司、辦公室英語、運動、喝下午茶、飯店、觀光...等，徜徉多采多姿的外國生活。

　　相信有趣又生活化的英語會話能夠讓您在輕鬆愉快的閱讀中，英文實力大提升。

Chapter1

家居生活

我是**英語會話王**
I am English Coversation King

Chapter2

享受美食

我是**英語會話王**
I am English Coversation King

Chapter3 · · · · · · · · ·

逛街

Chapter4

辦公用語

Chapter5

休閒旅遊

我是**英語會話王**
I am English Coversation King

Chapter6 · · · · · · · · · ·

單字補充

我是**英語會話王**
I am English Coversation King

Chapter7

生活常用句

CHAPTER
1

家居生活

In the Bedroom
➲ 在臥室

A It's time to get up.

該請床了。

B What time is it?

現在幾點?

A It is ten.

十點。

B Ooooh~~~

喔~~~

A Want me to wake you up later?

要我晚點叫你嗎?

B Ok, please wake me up in 10 minutes.

好,請在10分鐘之後叫醒我。

In the Living Room1

⮕ 在客廳1

A Good morning.

早安。

B Good morning. It's really a nice day, isn't it?

早安。今天天氣真好耶,是吧?

A Yeah, it's a sunny day.

是啊,陽光普照。

B A sunny holiday.

陽光普照的假日。

A Why don't we go for a drive today?

我們今天何不出去兜風?

In the Living Room2

➲ 在客廳2

A I'm going to cook a delicious breakfast this morning.

我今天早上要煮好吃的早餐。

B Really? For me?

真的？ 做給我吃嗎？

A Yes, for us.

是啊，給我們吃。

B Wow! Cool!

哇！好耶！

In the Kitchen

➲ 在廚房

A Are you washing the food?

你在洗菜嗎？

B Yes. Would you help me set the table?

是的。你可以幫我擺餐具嗎？

A Sure. What are you going to make for breakfast?

當然。你要做什麼早餐？

B Guess.

猜猜看。

A French toast?

法國吐司？

B Exactly. And something more. I will make

fried mushroom with basil first.

沒錯。還有更多。我要先做蘑菇炒九層塔。

A Wow, how can I help you?

哇,我該怎麼幫你?

B Please peel off the potatoes. I will boil them and slightly cook them with bacon and cream later.

請幫我削馬鈴薯。等一下我會先用水煮,再和培根、奶油一起煮。

A That sounds wonderful.

聽起來很棒。

B How do you like your eggs cooked? Fried sunny-side up, over, over-easy or scrambled?

你想要吃怎麼樣的蛋? 單面熟,雙面熟,嫩煎蛋,還是炒蛋?

A I'd like a scrambled egg, thank you!

■ 我想要炒蛋，謝謝！

B Milk or tea?
牛奶還是紅茶？

A I want milk tea!
我想要奶茶！

B No problem!
沒問題！

A What about you?
那你呢？

B Don't worry about me. I'll take care of it.
別擔心我。我來做就好。

At the table1

➜ 用餐時1

A Here we go!

來囉！

B You are so nice. Thank you!

你真好。謝謝！

A My pleasure.

我的榮幸。

B Delicious!

好吃！

A It tastes good?

好吃嗎？

B Yes, wonderful. I love you so much!

很好吃，我超愛你的！

At the table2

➔ 用餐時2

A Did you sleep well last night?

你昨晚睡得好嗎？

B Yes, good. And you?

嗯，很好。你呢？

A Yes. I even had a sweet dream.

嗯。我還做了一個好夢呢。

B Wow, may I know what the dream was about?

哇，我可以知道是什麼夢嗎？

A Mmm, secret.

嗯…秘密。

B Tell me now, please.

■ 告訴我嘛,拜託。

A OK. Well, you were also in the dream...
好吧。嗯,你也有出現在我夢中…

B And then?
然後呢?

A Ah... I'll tell you later.
呃…我晚些告訴你。

B What did I do in your dream?
我在你夢中做了什麼?

A Oh, the water is boiling!
喔,水滾了!

Questions Answers

➲ 一問一答

A What were they doing?

他們在做什麼？

B They were preparing the food.

他們在準備餐點。

A What are they doing?

他們在做什麼？

B They are having breakfast.

他們在吃早餐。

A Who cooked the breakfast?

誰煮了早餐？

B Mary cooked the breakfast.

瑪莉煮了早餐。

A Who set the table?

誰擺餐具？

B Tom set the table.

湯姆擺了餐具。

A Where is Mary?

瑪莉在哪裡？

B She is in the kitchen.

她在廚房。

A Where is Tony?

東尼在哪裡？

B He is in the living room.

他在客廳。

A Is he watching TV?

他在看電視嗎？

B No, he is listening to music and playing with his phone.

沒有，他在聽音樂玩手機。

A Is Jimmy still sleeping?

吉米在睡覺嗎？

B No, he is studying.

沒有，他在讀書。

A Who is on the phone?

誰在講電話？

B Amy is on the phone.

艾咪在講電話。

A What is Henry doing?

亨利在做什麼？

我是**英語會話王**
I am English Coversation King

B He is using his computer.
他在用電腦。

A Isn't he playing the guitar?
他不是在玩吉他嗎？

B No. he is not.
不，他沒有。

A Did you see our Kitty?
你有看見我們的咪咪嗎？

B She's sleeping on the sofa.
牠在沙發上睡覺。

In the Bathroom

➜ 在浴室

A Jane, are you taking a shower?

珍，妳在洗澡嗎？

B No.

沒有。

A I need to wash my hands.

我想要洗手。

B I'm brushing my teeth, wait a moment.

我在刷牙，等一下。

A Did you brush your hair yet?

妳有梳頭髮了嗎？

B Not yet.

還沒。

A Where are my glasses?

我的眼鏡呢？

B Aren't they on your desk?

沒有在妳的桌上嗎？

A No, I couldn't find them.

沒有，我找不到。

B Did you put them in the bathroom?

有放在浴室嗎？

A Oh, maybe.

喔，有可能。

In the House
➲ 在家中

A I have to do house work later.

我等一下必須要做家事。

B I can help you.
我可以幫你。

A I will clean up the table.

我會整理桌子。

B I will wash the dishes.
我會洗碗。

A I will take out the trash.

我會去倒垃圾。

B I will do the laundry.
我會去洗衣服。

我是**英語會話王**
I am English Coversation King

After cleaning

➲ 打掃完畢

A When are we going out today?

我們什麼時候出門？

B I'll take a shower first and get dressed, I guess 3 o'clock?

我會先洗個澡、著裝，應該3點吧？

A OK! Where are we going?

OK！我們要去哪兒？

B I have been longing for the seashore for a long time.

我已經想去海邊很久了。

A Really? Isn't the sea far from here?

真的？海不是離這裡很遠嗎？

B No, it only takes 15 minutes by car.
不會，開車只要15分鐘就到了。

A Great! Let's go to the seashore!
好棒！那我們去海邊！

B Don't forget your sun cream!
別忘了你的防曬乳唷！

A Sure. And sunglasses!
當然。還有墨鏡！

B Will you bring water?
你會帶水嗎？

A OK. I will.
好。我會帶。

Getting Ready

➡ 準備

A Are you coming down?

你要下來了嗎？

B Oh, I'm getting dressed, just a moment. Are you ready?

喔，我正在穿衣服。你已經好了？

A Yes, I am ready. Don't worry. Take your time.

是的，我好了。別著急。慢慢來。

B Here I am.

我來了。

A Wow, you look wonderful.

哇，好美。

At the Beach

➲ 在沙灘

A How beautiful it is!

好美！

B Clean sky, deep blue water. I love this feeling.

晴朗天空，深藍色海水。我愛這個感覺。

A Let's run to the water!

我們跑過去水那邊吧！

B Ha ha, wait for me!

哈哈，等我！

A The water is cool!

水很涼耶！

B Wow, cool!

我是**英語會話王**
I am English Coversation King

哇,酷!

A I am happy.
好開心。

B I feel relaxed.
好放鬆。

A I am excited.
好興奮。

B Hey, I don't want to get wet.
嘿,我不想弄濕身體。

A Me, either. But, have fun!
我也不想。不過, 玩一下嘛!

B Stop it! Come back!
住手!回來!

At the Seashore

➲ 在海邊

A They are splashing water on each other.

他們正在互相潑水。

B Yeah, it is the most interesting thing in the sea.

是啊,那是在海邊最好玩的事了。

A You mean it?

你是真心的嗎?

B Oh, well... walking along the beach is much better... wait! Stop it!

喔,嗯…在海邊散步還是比較好…等一下!停手!

A OK, OK... Why don't we paint on the

sand?

好啦，好啦…不然我們在沙灘上畫畫如何？

B Good idea.

好主意。

A Come here!

過來這邊！

B Wait for me!

等等我！

A Hurry!

快一點！

Coming Back Home

➲ 回家

A Did you have a good time?

玩得高興嗎？

B Yes, great!

嗯，很高興！

A I enjoyed today so much. How wonderful a day we have spent!

我今天玩得很高興。真的是美好的一天耶！

B You are right, I feel so happy.

是啊，我覺得很幸福。

A I think getting close to the nature is truly a happy thing.

■ 我覺得靠近大自然真的很幸福。

B Yes, I can't agree more.
是啊，我超級認同。

A Do you want to go to the mountains next time?
下次你想去登山嗎？

B Alright!
好哇！

A It's time to go to bed.
該睡了。

B It is still early.
還早啊。

A I need to sleep early, so that I can get up early tomorrow.
我得早點睡，這樣明天才能早起。

享受美食

At the restau-rant1

➔ 餐廳1

A Welcome. Please take your seat here. waitress will be with you later.

歡迎。請坐這邊。等一下會有服務生過來。

(5 minutes later / 5分鐘後)

A Are you ready for me to take your orders?

請問要點餐了嗎？

B Yes, I would like to have a steak, please.

可以，我想要牛排。

A How would you like it cooked?

請問要幾分熟？

B Medium.
五分熟。

A Would you like some desserts?
需要點心嗎？

B Yes, what kinds of dessert do you have?
要，你們有什麼點心？

A We have cheese cake, chocolate mousse and burnt cream.
我們有起司蛋糕、巧克力慕斯和烤布蕾。

B Please give me a chocolate mousse.
請給我巧克力慕斯。

In a Coffee Shop

➔ 咖啡廳

A What would you like to have?

請問要點什麼呢？

B An apple pie and an ice-cream waffle.

一份蘋果派和一份霜淇淋鬆餅。

A What kind of ice cream do you want?

要什麼口味的霜淇淋？

B What kind of ice cream do you have?

有什麼口味的霜淇淋？

A We have chocolate, vanilla and strawberry.

有巧克力、香草和草莓口味。

B Vanilla, please.
香草的，謝謝。

A Would you like to have something to drink?
請問要飲料嗎？

B Yes, please give us one milk tea, and one chocolate sorbet.
要，請給我們一杯奶茶，一杯巧克力冰沙。

A How would you like your milk tea? Iced or hot?
請問奶茶要冰的還是熱的？

B Hot, please.
請給我熱的。

Asking for a Date

⊃ 邀約

A Would you like to go out with me tonight?

你今天晚上有空嗎？

B Oh, sorry. I have a date already.
喔，抱歉。我已經有其他的約了。

A Will you be free this Saturday?

這星期六你有空嗎？

B I will be free at noon time on Saturday.
我星期六的中午有空。

A So would you like to have lunch with me?

■ 那你是否願意跟我一起共進午餐？

B Yes.
好。

A Good. Let's meet at the library at 11:30, will that be OK?
很好。那我們約11：30在圖書館見，可以嗎？

B Yes, OK.
可以，好的。

A OK. See you then.
好。到時候見。

At the restau-rant2

➲ 餐廳2

A Did you book a table?

有訂位嗎？

B Yes.

有。

A What is the name?

請問名字是？

B Martin.

馬汀。

A Yes, please come this way. Can I take your order now?

有的，請往這邊走。請問要點餐了嗎？

Track 16

B Please give us one more minute.
請再給我們一分鐘。

(5 minutes later / 5分鐘後)

B We are ready to order.
我們可以點餐了。

A What would you like to order?
請問要點什麼？

B Braised Lamb, Prawns and Sea Bass, please.
燉小羊肉，明蝦和鱸魚，謝謝。

A And for dessert?
甜點呢？

B Cake, please.
蛋糕。

A Anything else?

我是**英語會話王**
I am English Coversation King

■ 還有需要其他的嗎？

B That's all, thanks.
沒有了，謝謝。

A Here is your coffee.
這是您的咖啡。

B I didn't order a coffee.
我沒有點咖啡。

A Oh, sorry. You ordered iced tea and green tea, right?
喔，抱歉。您點的是冰茶和綠茶，是嗎？

B Yes.
是。

A Here you are.
在這邊。

(After 1 hour / 1小時後)

B Could I have the bill, please?

可以給我帳單嗎？

A That will be a total 20 of dollars.

總共是20美金。

B Is the service charge included?

有包含服務費嗎？

A Yes, tax and a 10% service charge are included.

有的，有包含10%的稅和服務費。

B Here you are.

在這裡。

我是**英語會話王**
I am English Coversation King

At the restaurant3

➲ 餐廳3

A Can I take your order?

請問要點餐了嗎？

B Yes. What are the specials?

好。本店特色餐是什麼？

A Tortellini is our special.

義大利方餃是我們的主打。

B OK, I will have one Tortellini.

好，那我要點一份義大利餃。

A To go or dine here?

這邊用還是帶走？

B Dine here.
這邊用。

A Anything to drink?
需要喝的嗎？

B What drinks do you have?
有什麼飲料？

A We have Cola, Cider and fresh squeezed orange juice.
有可樂，蘋果酒和現榨柳橙汁。

B I'll have fresh squeezed orange juice.
我要現榨柳橙汁。

我是**英語會話王**
I am English Coversation King

Track 18

In a Fast Food Resturant1

➲ 在速食餐廳1

A May I help you?

需要什麼嗎？

B I would like to have a burger.

我要一個漢堡。

A What kind of burger?

哪一種漢堡？

B Spicy chicken filet, please.

勁辣雞腿堡。

A What would you like to drink?

請問要喝什麼？

B Sprite. Thank you.
雪碧。謝謝。

A Would you like fries to go with that?
需要搭配薯條嗎？

B No, that's all. Thank you.
不用，這樣就可以了。

A It is 4 dollars and 30 cents.
這樣是4塊30分。

B Here you are.
在這邊。

A Here is your change and receipt.
這是您的零錢和發票。

In a Fast Food Resturant2

➜ 在速食餐廳2

A May I help you?

需要什麼嗎？

B I want combo 3.

我要3號餐。

A For here or to go?

這邊用還是帶走？

B For here.

這邊用。

A What would you like to drink?

請問要喝什麼？

B Iced tea.
冰茶。

A Do you want a large fries?
薯條要加大嗎？

B No, medium is ok.
不用，中薯就可以。

A Anything else?
還有其他需要嗎？

B No, that's all. Thank you.
沒有。這樣就好。謝謝。

我是**英語會話王**
I am English Coversation King

At the restau-rant4

➲ 餐廳4

A How many are in your group?

請問有幾位？

B 8 people.

8位。

A Do you have a reservation?

請問有訂位嗎？

B No. Do you have a table for 8 persons?

沒有。你們有八人的位置嗎？

A There will be one table available in 10 minutes. Would you like to wait?

有一桌再10分鐘就可以入座，請問願意等待嗎？

B OK. Could I see the menu first, please?

好。我可以先看菜單嗎？

A Here is the menu, Sir.

先生，這是菜單。

(After 10 minutes/過了10分鐘)

A The table is ready for you. Please come this way.

位置為您好了。請往這邊。

B Would you give us water, please?

可以給我們水嗎？

A Yes, sure.

好的。

B Can I order now?

可以點了嗎？

A What would you like to have?

■ 請問要用什麼？

B What do people order most?
　最多人點的是什麼？

A Lasagna Pizza is very popular.

千層披薩很受歡迎。

B Is it spicy?
　會辣嗎？

A No, it is a little salty.

不會，吃起來鹹鹹的。

B OK, We'll have a Lasagna Pizza, Spaghetti with Marinara Sauce, Cheese Ravioli, Tortellini, Grilled Shrimp, Strawberry Cheese Cake, Carrot Cake and one of this. By the way, what is Sobremesa maravilhosa?

好，我們要點一個千層披薩，義式番茄醬義大利麵，起司義大利方餃，義大利餃，烤蝦，草莓蛋

Track 20

糕、紅蘿蔔蛋糕和一個這個。對了，Sobremesa
maravilhosa(美妙甜點的葡萄牙文)是什麼？

A It means our special dessert and it is
tiramissu in a glass.

那是本店招牌點心的意思，是裝在玻璃杯裡面的
提拉米蘇。

B And, what is Grilled Cheese Hero?

Grilled Cheese Hero是什麼？

A It is sandwich with cheese, tomatos
and butter.

他是三明治裡面有起司、番茄和奶油。

B I see. So, that's all. Please make sure that
our meals are served without broccoli and
green beans.

我瞭解了。那這樣就好。我們的餐點請都不要放
花椰菜和青豆。

A OK, we will cook them without broccoli and green beans for you.

好，我們不會放花椰菜和青豆進去的。

B Please give me a towel.

請給我一條毛巾。

A Here you are.

在這邊。

B Please give me one more fork.

請再給我一支叉子。

A Sure, anything else?

好的，還有需要什麼嗎？

B I would like some more water.

我想要多一點水。

A Ok, I'll be right back.

好，馬上拿給您。

B Where is the restroom?
化妝室在哪裡？

A Please go in that direction and you will find it on your right side.

請往那個方向走，然後在右手邊就會看到。

(After 1 hour 1 / 小時之後)

B Check, please.
請給我們帳單。

A May I help you?

需要什麼嗎？

B Can we have our check, please?
可以給我們帳單？

A Yes, just a second.

好的，請稍等。

A That will be 170 dollars and 79 cents.

■ 總共是170塊79分。

B Is the service charge included?
有包含服務費嗎？

A Yes.
有。

B Here are 171 dollars. You can keep the change.
這邊是171塊。不用找了。

Making new friends

➲ 交朋友

A Hi.

嗨。

B Hi.

嗨。

A Can I join you for a drink?

我可以坐這邊和你喝飲料嗎？

B Yes.

可以。

A My name is Kevin, and yours?

我的名字是凱文，你呢？

我是**英語會話王**
I am English Coversation King

B I'm Rose.
我是玫瑰。

A Are you here for a visit?
你來這裡觀光嗎？

B No.
不是。

A It's my first time visiting London.
這是我第一次拜訪倫敦。

B Are you traveling alone?
你一個人來旅行嗎？

A I'm on a business trip, and I will leave London next Monday.
我是來出差的，我下星期一就要離開倫敦了。

B Did you go sightseeing yet?
你有去觀光了嗎？

A No actually. Where do you suggest?

不算有。你有建議的地方嗎？

B I think taking a Thames River cruise is good.

我覺得搭泰晤士河的遊艇很不錯。

A I wish that I will have time to see it.

我希望我會有時間去。

B You will.

你會的。

A I hope so.

但願如此。

In a Bank

➲ 在銀行

A How can I help you?

請問要辦什麼業務？

B I need to exchange some currency.
我要換錢。

A What currency would you like to change?

要換什麼幣別？

B NT Dollars into US Dollars.
新台幣換美金。

A The exchange rate is... 30.8 now, and there will be a handling charge of 7 dollars. Will that be OK?

現在匯率是30.8，會扣掉7塊錢美金的手續費，這

■ 樣可以嗎？

B Yes, that's OK.
可以。

A How much would you like to change?
請問要換多少？

B I'd like to change 10 thousand NT Dollars. Here it is.
我想要換台幣一萬塊。在這邊。

A Yes, it is 10 thousand NT Dollars. So, here is 317 US Dollars and 67 cents for you. Please check and sign your name here.

沒錯，這裡是台幣一萬塊。好，這邊是美金317元67分。請確認，然後在這邊簽名。

B Yes. That's right. Thank you.
好的。沒有錯。謝謝。

相關句子Related Wordings

☑ I want to have something delicious.

我想吃點美味的東西。

☑ Can we have the bill, please?

可以我們帳單嗎？

☑ Do you have non-caffeinated non-alcoholic drinks?

請問有不含咖啡因和酒精的飲料嗎？

☑ Which one tests better?

哪一種比較好喝？

☑ Which drink is the best seller?

哪種飲料最有人氣？

☑ Please recommend one.

請推薦。

☑ Is this sweet?

這個會甜嗎？

☑ How does this taste?

是什麼味道？

☑ It is too sweet.

這個太甜了。

☑ It's sweet.

甜甜的。

☑ It's sour.

酸酸的。

☑ It's bitter.

苦苦的。

☑ It's spicy.

辣辣的。

☑ Would you give me a straw?

請給我吸管。

☑ One bubble tea.

　一杯珍珠奶茶。

☑ One ice-cream waffle.

　一份霜淇淋鬆餅。

☑ One apple pie, one doughnut, and two cups of black tea.

　一份蘋果派，一個甜甜圈，兩杯紅茶。

☑ Do you like them with ice or hot?

　要熱的還是冰的？

☑ Iced.

　冰的。

☑ I would like to get a refill.

　我要續杯。

☑ May I help you?

　需要什麼嗎？

☑ I would like juice.

請給我果汁。

☑ Two ice-cream cones.

兩個霜淇淋甜筒。

☑ How about having some tea and we can talk about this issue?

我們一邊喝飲料一邊談這事如何？

☑ Please give me a glass of water.

請給我一杯水。

☑ Would you give me an empty glass?

請給我一個杯子。

☑ Do you use fresh ground coffee or instant coffee?

請問你們的是現煮咖啡還是即溶式咖啡？

☑ We use fresh ground coffee only.

我們只用現煮咖啡。

I am English
Coversation King

逛街

Track 25

Clothes Store1

➲ 服飾店1

A Hello, may I help you?

哈囉，需要什麼嗎？

B Yes, I'm looking for a jacket.

恩，我在找夾克。

A Here are our jackets. How about this one?

我們的夾克在這邊。這一件如何？

B It's nice. Can I try it on?

不錯。我可以試穿嗎？

A Yes, sure. The changing room is over there.

可以。試衣間在那邊。

B It's a little bit too tight. Do you have a larger size?

有一點太緊了。有大一點的尺寸嗎？

A Yes, here you are.

有的，在這邊。

B How much is it?

這件多少？

A It is 10 dollars.

10塊錢。

B Any discount?

有折扣嗎？

A No, sorry.

沒有，抱歉。

B Ok, I'll take it.

好，我買了。

我是**英語會話王**
I am English Coversation King

In a Outlet1

➲ 暢貨中心1

A Coach bags are much cheaper here than in Taiwan.

Coach包包，比台灣還要便宜很多耶。

B There are a lot of brand shops here, and they are really cheap.

這邊有很多名牌店，而且很便宜。

A For example?

例如？

B GAP, AF, HM, Holister, Forever21, American Eagle, Pandora, Calvin Klein, Tiffany, NIKE and so on.

GAP, AF, HM, Holister, Forever21, American Eagle, Pandora, Calvin Klein, Tiffany, NIKE等等。

A Wow, can we see them all in this outlet?

哇，在這家暢貨中心全部都有？

B Almost. If you have a favorite brand, tell me, I will take you there.

幾乎。如果你有喜歡的牌子，告訴我，我帶你過去。

A Thank you. You are so sweet.

謝謝，你好貼心喔。

B Why don't we take a look in Coach first?

我們要不要先看一下Coach呢？

A I've been wanting a beautiful real brand bag for a long time.

我已經想要一個真的名牌漂亮包包很久了。

B Now it's your best chance!

現在正是你的大好機會！

A By the way, how about CHANEL, ANNA SUI ,LV, GUCCI, FENDI, PRADA, GUESS, Versace, DKNY? Are they much cheaper here than in Taiwan?

對了，那香奈兒、ANNA SUI , LV, GUCCI, FENDI, PRADA, GUESS, Versace, DKNY呢？在這邊也比台灣便宜很多嗎？

B I'm not sure, maybe we should surf the internet, making sure everything first and then go on a shopping spree!

我不確定。或許我們應該先上網搜尋確認之後來個大血拼！

A Great idea!

好主意！

B So let's just do window shopping today.

那我們今天就先看一看就好囉。

A But, I think this is so worth buying Don't you think so? Isn't it beautiful? Look at the price!

可是，我覺得這個很值得買耶。你不覺得嗎？是不是很漂亮？你看它的價格！

B I have a member card in this outlet, let me see if there are any coupons that we can use...

我在這家暢貨中心有會員卡，我查查看有沒有什麼優惠券可以使用…

A Coupons?

優惠券？

B Yeah, sometimes they have sales discount... but no, not these days.

是啊，有時候會有拍賣打折，喔不，這幾天沒有。

A That's OK. Martin, do you think this bag goes well with me?

沒關係。馬汀，你覺得這個包包適合我嗎？

B Mmm.

嗯…

Track 26

A I like these 3, which one do you like best?

我喜歡這3個，你覺得哪一個最好看？

B I like you with this one.

我喜歡你拿這一個。

A Does it go well with me?

跟我很搭嗎？

B Yes.

很搭。

A Ok, I'll take it.

好，那我要買了。

At the check-out counter

➲ 結帳

A Excuse me. How much is this?

不好意思。請問這多少？

B It is 102.8 dollars.

102塊80分。

A Do you have an international discount?

你們有觀光客折扣嗎？

B Yes, please show me your passport.

有的，請給我看您的護照。

B Ok, you will get 10% off, and it will be 92.52 dollars. Cash or credict card?

好的，為您打9折，這樣是92塊52分，現金或是刷卡？

In a Outlet2

➲ 暢貨中心2

A Let's go.

走吧。

B I haven't paid yet.

我還沒付錢耶。

A I paid. It's a present for you.

我付了。是送你的禮物。

B Oh, Martin, thank you, thank you.

喔，馬汀。謝謝，謝謝。

In a department store

➲ 百貨公司

A Need any help?

有什麼需要的嗎？

B I am looking for a skirt.

我在找裙子。

A Casual or formal?

要正式的或休閒的？

B For an interview.

面試時要穿的。

A How about this?

這件如何？

我是**英語會話王**
I am English Coversation King

B I will take a look around first.
我先逛一下。

A Take your time.
慢慢看。

B Do you have this in any other colors?
請問這件有別的顏色嗎？

A Yes. Here they are.
有的，在這邊。

B I like the blue one. May I try it on?
我喜歡藍色的。可以試穿嗎？

A Yes. What is your size?
可以，請問您的尺寸多少？

B M.
M號。

A Is it 36?

是36嗎？

B I don't know.

我不知道。

A That is OK. Please try this on first.

沒關係。請試穿這件。

B Do you have a bigger size? I want to try both of them.

有更大一點的尺寸嗎？我想要兩件都試穿。

(3 minutes later / 3分鐘後)

A How does it fit?

合身嗎？

B This one fits me well.

這件衣服剛好合身。

A You look really nice in it.

■ 真是太適合您了。

B But I think it's too long for me.
但是我覺得有點太長了。

A Don't worry. We provide free alteration service.
別擔心，我們有免費修改的服務。

 相關句子Related Wordings

Track 29

☑ Do you have a bigger size?
有大一號的嗎？

☑ Do you have a smaller size?
有小一號的嗎？

☑ Please give me a smaller size.
請給我小一號的。

☑ May I help you?

需要幫忙嗎？

☑ I'll just look around first.

我先看看就好。

☑ Do you have skirts?

有裙子嗎？

☑ Where can I see the pants?

長褲在哪邊？

☑ How can I help you?

需要幫忙嗎？

☑ I need clothes for office work.

我想找上班穿的衣服。

☑ I suggest a skirt and a blouse.

我建議您買裙子和襯衫。

☑ What is the new style?

最近流行的款式是什麼？

☑ I want to buy a suit.

我想要買套裝。

☑ I am looking for a T-shirt.

我在找T恤。

☑ Where is the jewelry department?

珠寶專櫃區在哪邊？

☑ It is on the 1 floor.

在一樓。

☑ Where is CHANEL?

香奈爾在哪裡？

Track 30

☑ Please introduce the perfume to me.

請給我看香水。

☑ Where can I find menswear?

請問男性服飾在哪裡？

☑ Where is the information counter?

詢問台在哪邊 ?

☑ May I put my suitcase here?

行李可以放在這邊嗎 ?

☑ Would you keep my suitcase here?

可以幫我保管行李嗎 ?

☑ Where are the lockers?

置物櫃在哪裡 ?

☑ I did not see anything I like.

沒有特別喜歡的。

☑ May I take a look here?

我可以逛一下嗎 ?

☑ Please show me that one.

請給我看那個。

☑ May I try it on?

這可以試穿嗎 ?

☑ I want to exchange this.

請幫我換成別的。

☑ When did you buy it?

什麼時候買的？

☑ I bought it here 3 days ago.

三天前在這裡買的。

☑ Is it possible to return or exchange something?

這邊可以退換貨嗎？

☑ Within how many days is it possible to exchange or return?

幾天之內可以換貨退貨？

Track 31

☑ I want to exchange it for a smaller size.

我想換小一號的。

☑ I want to exchange.

我想換貨。

☑ I bought it here yesterday. Can I return it?

我是昨天買的可以退貨嗎？

☑ Yes, have you brougt the receipt with you?

可以，有帶發票嗎？

☑ I did not use it at all.

我完全沒有用過。

☑ I bought this in another branch, may I exchange it here?

我在其他分店買的，可以在這家店換貨嗎？

☑ How much is the discount?

打幾折？（降價幾%？）

☑ It is 20% off.

打8折。（降價20%）

☑ Is this the price after the discount?

這個價格是打折價嗎？

☑ When will there be a sale?

拍賣什麼時候會開始？

☑ Next Saturday.

下星期六開始。

☑ How long will the sales last?

拍賣期間多久？

☑ One week.

一個星期。

☑ There is an activity of buy one get one free now.

現在有買一送一活動。

☑ It's buy two get one free.

現在買二送一。

☑ Give me a discount and I'll get it.

算我便宜一點我就買。

Track 32

☑ The total is fifty seven dollars and twenty eight cents.

總共是57.28元。

☑ Do you take credit cards?

可以用信用卡付嗎？

☑ Yes, would you like to pay cash in full or on an installment plan?

可以，請問要一次付清還是分期付款？

☑ Pay in full.

一次付清。

☑ Would you sign here?

可以請您在這邊簽名嗎？

☑ OK.

好。

☑ Where is the counter?

要在哪裡結帳？

☑ I think it is expensive.

我覺得很貴。

☑ Things in Taiwan are so cheap.

台灣的東西好便宜啊。

☑ I would like to visit the 101 building.

我想參觀101大樓。

Buying Clothes

➲ 買衣服

A Excuse me.

請問 (叫服務員)

B Yes?

是的。

A How much is this?

這個多少？

B It is 30 dollars.

美金30元。

A May I try?

我可以試穿看看嗎？

B Yes.

好，可以的。

我是**英語會話王**
I am English Coversation King

Track 33

A Where is the fitting room?

試衣間在哪裡？

B This way.

這邊。

A How many pieces?

請問試穿幾件？

B Three.

三件。

A How do they fit?

穿得合適嗎？

B This one is too small. And these are too long, do you provide free alteration service?

這件太小了。這兩件太長，你們有免費修改衣服的服務嗎？

Track 34

相關句子Related Wordings

☑ It doesn't fit me.

尺寸不合。

☑ Can I have the next size up?

我可以拿大件一點的嗎？

☑ Please give me one size bigger.

請給我大一號的尺寸。

☑ Please give me one size smaller.

請給我小一號的尺寸。

☑ Do you have other colors?

有其他顏色嗎？

☑ Yes, there arc also white, blue, and pink.

有，還有白色、藍色和粉紅色。

☑ It is too small.

太小了。

我是**英語會話王**
I am English Coversation King

☑ It is too big.

太大了。

☑ It just fits me!

很合身耶。

☑ Too tight.

太緊了。

☑ It is too long.

太長了。

☑ How do I look?

我看起來如何？

☑ Do you like it?

你喜歡這件嗎？

☑ I'll take it.

我要這件。

☑ Which color do you prefer?

你比較喜歡哪個顏色？

☑ Your dress looks expensive.

你的衣服看起來很貴。

☑ I got it for 3 dollars.

我用3塊美金買到的。

☑ What a bargain!

太物美價廉了吧！

☑ I want a red one.

我想要紅色的。

☑ I want a lighter color.

我想要淡一點的顏色。

☑ Do you have pale colors?

有淡色系列的嗎？

☑ I would like it in deep color.

我想要深色的。

☑ I like colorful ones.

我喜歡鮮豔的顏色。

☑ It suits you well.

很適合呢。

☑ You look great in it.

看起來很好。

☑ You look beautiful.

很漂亮。

☑ What is it made of?

這是甚麼材質？

☑ Cotton.

棉質。

☑ It's not suitable for me.

不太適合我。

☑ The tops are not allowed to try.

上衣不能試穿喔。

☑ So so.

普通耶。

☑ Too tight.

有點緊。

☑ This pants are too long.

褲子太長。

Track 36

☑ I need some hair pins.

我想買髮夾。

☑ I want to see necklaces.

有項鍊嗎？

☑ Can I try it on?

項鍊可以試戴嗎？

☑ Do you have necklace with earrings set?

有項鍊耳環組嗎？

我是英語會話王
I am English Coversation King

☑ Please pack them as a gift.

請包裝成禮物。

☑ Please pack them seperatly.

請幫我分開包裝。

☑ I want to buy a purse.

我要買皮包。

☑ Is this real?

這個是真品嗎？

☑ Is this real leather?

這是真皮嗎？

☑ Welcome. May I help you?

歡迎光臨。請問要找什麼？

☑ I would like to see cameras.

我想看相機。

☑ Looking for something?

請問要找什麼？

☑ I'm just looking around.

我只是看看。

☑ I will take a look for a second.

我先看一下。

☑ I would like to see the purse.

我想要買皮夾。

Track 37

☑ Do you have the cases for smart phone?

這邊有智慧型手機的殼嗎？

☑ Please show me.

請給我看。

☑ Can I try on this watch?

手錶可以試戴嗎？

☑ Is it water-proofed?

有防水嗎？

我是**英語會話王**
I am English Coversation King

Track 37

☑ It is on sale now.

現在正在打折中。

☑ It is sold out.

都賣完了。

☑ Can I come in?

我可以進去嗎？

☑ Please show me others.

請給我看別的。

☑ Would you show me how to use it?

可以示範給我看怎麼使用嗎？

☑ Can I touch it?

我可以摸摸看嗎？

☑ Do you have other ones?

沒有別的嗎？

☑ What colors do you prefer?

您想要哪種色調的？

☑ Do you have a pink one?

有粉紅色的嗎？

☑ Yes, we have a pink one.

是，有的。

☑ Is this the only type?

只有這種樣式嗎？

☑ Please show me other colors.

請給我看別種顏色。

Track 38

☑ Please show me the blue one.

請給我看藍色的。

☑ Do you have a bigger size?

這個有大一點的尺寸嗎？

☑ Do you have others similar to this?

有和這個相似的樣式嗎？

我是英語會話王
I am English Coversation King

Track 38

☑ Can I buy just one of them?

這可以單買嗎?

☑ I need to think about it.

我再想想看。

☑ I'll be back later.

我再逛一逛再來。

☑ I'll come back next time.

我下次再來。

☑ Excuse me...

請問…

☑ Hi, there.

老闆。

☑ Check, please.

我要付帳。

☑ Please show me high heels.

請給我看高跟鞋。

☑ I'm looking for sneakers.

我在找運動鞋。

☑ I'm looking for some comfortable shoes for casual wear.

我在找平常可以穿舒適的鞋子。

☑ I need a pair of comfortable shoes.

我想要舒適的鞋。

☑ I'm looking for low heels.

我在找低跟的鞋子。

☑ Please come this way.

請往這邊走。

Track 39

☑ May I try these on?

我可以試穿看看嗎？（鞋子）

☑ What is your size?

是什麼尺寸？

☑ They are too small.

太小。

☑ They are too big.

太大了。

☑ Do you have a bigger size?

有更大一點的嗎？

☑ Do you have a smaller size?

有更小一點的嗎？

☑ May I see other styles?

有其他款式嗎？

☑ Do you have them in other colors?

有其他顏色嗎？

☑ Is it made of real leather?

這個是真皮的嗎？

☑ Is this real NIKE?

這是真的NIKE嗎？

☑ They are beautiful.
很漂亮。

☑ They are comfortable.
很舒服。

☑ They are a little bit small.
鞋子有點小。

☑ They are a little too big.
鞋子有點大。

☑ How much is it?
這個多少？

☑ It's expensive.
很貴。

☑ Do you have a discount on it?
有打折嗎？

☑ Can I get any discount?

可以打折嗎？

☑ Please give me a discount.

請給我打折。

☑ I'll buy these.

我要買這些。

Cosmetics store

➲ 美妝店

A How may I help you?

需要什麼嗎？

B My skin is dry. I need a moisturizer.

我的皮膚很乾。我需要滋潤乳液。

A I suggest you use this cream. It contains honey and rose oil. What is your skin type?

我建議您用這款乳霜。它含有蜂蜜和玫瑰油。您是哪一種類型的肌膚？

B Combination and sensitive.

混合性加上敏感性。

A This one is for sensitive skin. It is natural and does no harm to your skin.

這款是給敏感性肌膚使用的，成分很天然不會傷害肌膚。

B May I try?
我可以試用嗎？

A Yes, pad it slightly...
可以，這樣輕輕拍上…

B I want to try some on my face.
我想要試一些在臉上。

A Sure, please do.
當然，請用。

B I would also like to see this.
我也想看這個。

A Here you are.
請看。

B Is this essence?

Track 40

■ 這是精華液嗎？

A Yes, it is essence with rich Vitamin C.

是的，這是精華液，含有豐富的維生素C。

B Which is more suitable for me?

哪一種比較適合我？

A I think cream is more suitable for your skin and the essence will also be good for your skin when you use it before you sleep.

我覺得滋潤雙比較適合你的肌膚，精華液在睡前使用也會對肌膚很好。

B OK... I will take this one.

好…我買這個。

Duty free

➲ 免稅商店

A May I help you?

需要幫忙嗎?

B I want to buy cosmetics.

我想買化妝品。

A What cosmetics do you want?

您想要哪種化妝品?

B I'm looking for foundation.

我在找粉底霜。

A Do you know BB Cushion?

您知道氣墊式粉餅嗎?

B What is that?

那是什麼?

A It is a new product which includes foundation, essence... would you like to try?

那是一款新產品，包含了粉底液，精華液…要試試看嗎？

B Yes, but please try it on my hand.

好，但是請塗在我手上。

A Sure.

好的。

B Also I want a lipstick.

我還想要唇膏

A Here are our lipsticks.

這邊是我們的唇膏。

B I want lipstick with good moisture.

我想要滋潤一點的唇膏。

A I recommend you try this. It is the most moisture kind of lipstick which can also be used as lip balm.

我建議您用這個。這款是最滋潤的唇膏，可以當作護唇膏使用。

B Can I try?

可以試用嗎？

A Yes. Beautiful.

可以。漂亮。

B Would you introduce me to more new and hot products?

你可以介紹我更多新的熱門產品嗎？

 相關句子Related Wordings

Track 42

☑ Clean your hands first.

請先洗手。

按摩臉部。

☑ Are you looking for something?

請問要找什麼商品嗎？

☑ I'll look around first.

我先逛一下。

☑ I'm looking for skin care.

我在找護膚產品。

☑ I need facial cream.

我需要面霜。

☑ Please recommend a mascara to me.

請推薦睫毛膏。

☑ What is the best seller?

賣得最好的商品是什麼？

Track 43

☑ I need facial lotion. Which one do you recommend?

我需要臉部乳液，你推薦哪一種？

我是**英語會話王**
I am English Coversation King

☑ What is your skin type?

您是哪種皮膚類型？

☑ Sensitive.

敏感性肌膚。

☑ Dry.

乾性肌膚。

☑ Oily.

油性肌膚。

☑ Combination.

混合性肌膚。

☑ When is it's expiry date?

保存期間是多久？

☑ I'll take this.

我要買這個。

☑ I want natural products.

我都用天然成分的產品。

☑ I'm looking for perfume.

我在找香水。

☑ I need some mask packs.

我在找面膜。

☑ I am looking for color kit.

請給我化妝組。

☑ Does it have a tester?

有試用品嗎？

☑ Do you have any tester gifts?

有試用的贈品嗎？

☑ Can I take this with me on the plane?

可以帶上飛機嗎？

☑ Which one is most popular?

最有人氣的是哪一種？

☑ Is it made in the USA?

這是美國製造的嗎？

☑ Where can I see its produced location?

製造地點寫在哪裡？

Track 44

In a Salon

➲ 美髮沙龍

☑ I'd like my hair cut.

我想剪頭髮。

☑ I'd like my hair dyed.

我想要染髮。

☑ I want a new hairdo.

我想換髮型。

☑ I want this hair style.

我想要這個髮型。

☑ How much is it to have a haircut?

剪髮是多少元？

☑ Please cut and dye my hair.

請幫我染色和剪髮。

我是**英語會話王**
I am English Coversation King

☑ I want brown waved hair.

我想要有波浪的褐色頭髮。

☑ Is it OK?

滿意嗎？

Track 45

☑ No, it's not OK.

不。我不滿意。

☑ No, it's so so.

不。我覺得很普通。

☑ Yes, it's good.

嗯，滿意。

☑ I want straight hair.

我想要直髮。

☑ I want curled hair.

我想要捲髮。

☑ I want waved hair.

我想要波浪捲。

☑ You have your hair cut?

你剪頭髮了？

☑ You have changed your hair style?

你換髮型了？

☑ Did you dye your hair?

你染髮了？

☑ I have got a new hair style, how's it?

我換新髮型了。如何？

☑ Excellent!

超好看！

☑ Wonderful!

美！

☑ Beautiful.

很美。

☑ You look so nice!

很好看！

☑ Handsome!

帥！

Checkout counter

➲ 結帳櫃台

A Please count this also.

這個也一起算。

B It seems something went wrong. What is this for?

好像有算錯喔。這個金額是什麼？

A It is 8.27 dollars for a blue jean.

這是牛仔褲8. 27元。

B I didn't buy a blue jean.

我沒有買牛仔褲。

A I'm sorry, I'll check for you again. It will be 20.23 in total. Please check if everything is right.

很抱歉。我重新幫您確認一次。這樣總共是20塊23分。請看看是否正確。

B Yes, that's right.

是的,對了。

A Sorry for the mistake, and thank you for coming. Wish you enjoy your day.

很抱歉剛才打錯了,謝謝光臨。祝您玩得愉快。

B That's OK. Thank you.

沒關係。謝謝。

 相關句子Related Wordings

Track 47

☑ Would you pack it as a gift?

可以幫我包裝成禮物嗎?

☑ Please give me the receipt.

請給我收據。

☑ Is tax included?

有含稅嗎？

☑ This price is wrong.

這邊金額錯了。

☑ The total amount is wrong.

合計錯了。

☑ You did not give me enough change.

找的錢不夠喔。

☑ The amount is incorrect. Please check again.

金額錯了。請再確認一次金額。

☑ I did, but not this.

我有，但不是這個。

☑ Where is the lost-and-found?

失物招領處在哪裡？

☑ I lost my purse.

我遺失了皮包。

☑ Do you have lockers here?

請問置物櫃在哪裡？

☑ There is an information desk. Please ask them.

請跟詢問台詢問。

☑ How much?

多少？

☑ Any discount?

有打折嗎？

☑ Don't you have any discount?

沒有打折嗎？

☑ Too expensive.

好貴。

☑ Give me a better price.

給我好一點的價錢。

☑ This is the best price.

這已經是最好的價格了。

☑ 300 dollars, and I'll take it.

算我300美金,我就買。

I am English
Coversation King

CHAPTER 4

辦公用語

interview1

➔ 面試1

A I'm here for the interview.

我是來面試的。

B What's your name?

你的名字是什麼？

A My name is Kate.

我的名字是凱特。

B Who are you seeing?

是跟誰約呢？

A I'm seeing Mr. Simpson the sales department manager.

我是跟業務部經理辛普森先生約的。

B Just take a seat here.

Track 48

■ 請先坐這邊。

A Thank you.

■ 謝謝。

B Do you like a cup of water or tea?

■ 你需要一杯水或者茶嗎？

A Water, please.

■ 水，謝謝。

我是**英語會話王**
I am English Coversation King

Interview 2

⊃ 面試2

A Have you been waiting long?

你等很久了吧？

B No, That's OK.

不會，沒關係。

A It is nice to meet you.

很高興見到你。

B Nice to meet you, too. I'm glad for this opportunity.Would you see my resume?

我也很高興見到你。很高興有這個機會。

您是否要看一下我的履歷呢？

A Yes.

好。

B Here is my resume.
這是我的履歷。

A Where was your last job?
你的上一份工作是什麼？

B I was working in ABC company.
我的上一份工作是在ABC公司。

A Why did you leave the job?
你為什麼離開那個公司？

B Because I moved to Taiwan.
因為我搬家來台灣。

A Tell me more about yourself.
告訴我更多關於妳自己。

Office day

➲ 上班日

A Good morning.

早安。

B Good morning.

早安。

(ring ring ring鈴鈴鈴)

A Is this Kate?

是凱特嗎？

B Yes, this is Kate speaking.

是的，我是凱特。

A Kate, will you come to my office now?

凱特你現在可以來我辦公室嗎？

B Yes, I'll be there in a moment.
好的，我馬上過去。

A By the way, bring me a cup of coffee, thank you.
順便幫我泡杯咖啡，謝謝。

B Yes. How would you like the coffee?
好的。要怎麼樣的咖啡？

A With sugar and double cream.
有糖，兩球奶精。

Answering Tele-phone Call 1

➔ 接電話1

A Hello, this is GR company.

為，這裡是GR公司。

B I would like to speak to Mr. Simpson.

請幫我轉辛普森先生。

A Could I ask who is calling, please?

可以請問您是誰嗎？

B Yes, my name is Loren Cruise.

好，我是Loren Cruise。

A Ok, please hold on the line.

好，請等一下。

Answering Telephone Call 2

➔ 接電話2

A Mr. Simpson , you have Ms. Loren Cruise on line 3.

辛普森先生，勞倫·克魯絲小姐來電找您，她在 3線。

B No, I don't want to talk to her.

不，我不想跟她說話。

A Should I tell her that you are busy and will call her back later?

要不要我告訴她您在忙，晚一點回電給她？

B Tell her that I am not in the office.

告訴她我不在公司。

Ⓐ Yes, I will tell her that you are not in the office.

好，我告訴她您不在公司。

(pick up the phone again再次拿起電話)

Ⓐ Hello? Ms. Cruise, I'm sorry that Mr. Simpson is not in office today.

喂？克魯絲女士，很抱歉辛普森先生今天不在辦公室。

Ⓒ Will you tell him that I'm looking for him?

你可以跟他說我在找他嗎？

Ⓐ Yes, sure. I will.

好的，當然。我會跟他說的。

Answering Telephone Call 3

➲ 接電話3

A Can I speak with Mr. Simpson?

我想跟辛普森先生說話。

B I'm sorry, he is in a meeting right now.

不好意思,他現在正在開會。

A Do you mind if I ask who I am speaking with?

我可以請教您是誰嗎?

B My name is Kate, I am Mr. Simpson's new secretary.

我是凱特,辛普森先生的新秘書。

A Nice to meet you, Kate.

我是英語會話王
I am English Coversation King

■ 很高興認識你，凱特。

A Would you like to leave a message or call again later?

您想要留言或者晚一點再打嗎？

B Please leave a message for me, and ask Mr. Simpson to call me back.

請幫我留言，請辛普森先生回電給我。

A I'll tell him as soon as he finishes his meeting. Could I know who is calling, please?

他會議一結束我就告訴他。請問您是哪一位？

B This is Ken from BBC company.

我是BBC公司的肯。

A What is it about?

請問是什麼事情？

B He knows, just let him call me and that will

be OK.
他知道，你只要請他回電就可以了。

A OK.
好的。

B Thank you, bye.
謝謝，掰。

A Bye.
掰。

Scheduling

➲ 安排行程

A Hello, may I speak to Mr. Jo?

喂，請問裴先生在嗎？

B This is Mr. Jo's office, and I am Mr. Jo's secretary. You could just speak to me.

這裡是裴先生的辦公室，我是他的秘書，您可以直接跟我說。

A Mr. Simpson would like to schedule a meeting with Mr. Jo.

辛普森先生想要約時間和裴先生見面。

B What time will he be free?

他什麼時候有空呢？

A Next Tuesday 2PM, will Mr. Jo be free then?

■ 下星期二下午2點， 那時候裴先生有空嗎？

B Let me check... yes, Next Tuesday 2PM will be fine.

我看一下…可以的，下星期二下午2點可以。

A Ok, so we will meet Mr. Jo in your company then.

好，那我們會去貴公司與裴先生見面。

Hosting the Visiters

➲ 接待訪客

A Would you like some coffee or tea?

您想要來點咖啡或是茶嗎？

B Yes, thank you.

好，謝謝。

A Do you prefer coffee or tea?

您想要咖啡或是茶？

B Coffee, please.

咖啡，謝謝。

A How would you like your coffee?

您想要怎麼樣的咖啡？

B With sugar and milk.
我要加糖和牛奶的。

A Would you like some coffee or tea?
您想要來點咖啡或是茶嗎？

C Tea, please.
茶，謝謝。

A What kind of tea do you like, black tea or green tea?
要什麼茶呢，紅茶還是綠茶？

C Black tea, please.
請給我紅茶。

A Would you like it iced or hot?
要冰的還是熱的？

C Iced, thank you.
冰的，謝謝。

Booking a Table

➲ 餐廳訂位

A Hello, I'd like to book a table for next Friday night for 10 people.

喂，我想要訂下星期五晚上10個人的位置。

B Ok, what time will you be arrived?

好的，請問幾點到？

A 7 o'clock.

7點。

B Ok, what is the name , please?

好，請問大名是？

A Leon William.

里昂威廉。

B Ok, we have your booking.

好的，我們會為您預留位置。

A Thank you.

謝謝。

B Would you like to order now?

請問您要先點餐嗎？

A No. We will order then.

不了。我們到時候再點。

我是**英語會話王**
I am English Coversation King

Answering Telephone Call 4

➲ 接電話4

A Kate?

凱特？

B Yes, this is Kate speaking.

是，我是凱特。

A Did you send me the quotation yet?

你寄給我報價單了沒？

B Yes, Mr. Jason, I sent you the quotation via email this morning at 10:30.

有的，傑森先生，我今天上午10:30用email寄報價單給您了。

A Is it an excel file?

是excel檔嗎？

B Yes, it is an excel file named QUOTATION 20150601.

是的，是excel檔名稱是QUOTATION20150601。

A But I did not receive the email you sent. What is the title of your email?

但是我沒有收到你的email。 你email的主旨是什麼？

B QUOTATION 20150601.

QUOTATION 20150601。

A I couldn't find it.

找不到耶。

B Mr. Jason, may I confirm your email again? I sent it to js.good@samsung.co.kr , is that correct?

傑森先生，我可以跟您確認您的email位址嗎？我寄到js.good@samsung.co.kr，這是對的嗎？

A No, it's wrong. My email is js.good@ samsung.com

■ 不,不對。我的email是js. good@samsung. com。

B Oh, I see. I am sorry.

不 喔,我瞭解。抱歉。

A That is OK, send to me as soon as possible.

沒關係。盡快寄給我。

B I just sent the quotation to you, would you check again?

我剛才把報價單寄給您了,您可以在確認一次嗎?

A I got it now.

現在收到了。

B Thank you.

謝謝。

A I will take a look of It and reply to you.

我會看一下再回覆你。

B Yes, thank you.
好的，謝謝。

我是**英語會話王**
I am English Coversation King

Computer problem

➔ 電腦問題

A My mouse doesn't work.

我的滑鼠不會動了。

B Is it well-plugged?

線有插好嗎？

A Yes.

有。

B Why don't you try replugging it?

拔起來再插一次呢？

A Ok, I did. But it still doesn't work.

好。再插一次了。但是一樣不會動。

Track 58

B Close your windows. You have to reset your computer.
把視窗關一關。可能要重開機了。

A Files all saved?
檔案都要儲存嗎？

B Yes.
要。

(push the reset button按下重開機鈕)

B Does it work?
會動了嗎？

A Yes, it works! Thank you!
會，會動了！謝謝！

B No problem!
別客氣。

我是**英語會話王**
I am English Coversation King

Chatting1

⊃ 聊天1

A You look great in suits.

你穿西裝很好看耶。

B Thank you.

謝謝。

A Why don't you wear like this every-day?

你怎麼不每天都穿這樣?

B You really like it, uh?

你真的很喜歡我穿這樣,厚?

A Yes, you are so handsome in suits.

是啊,你穿西裝很帥。

B Do women like men in suits best?

Track 59

■ 女生最喜歡男生穿西裝嗎？

A For me, it is true. How about men? What clothes do you think women are most beautiful?

就我而言，沒錯。那男生呢？ 你們覺得女生穿什麼最漂亮？

B I think women are most beautiful in dress or suits.

我覺得女生穿洋裝或者套裝時最漂亮。

A I see.

我瞭解了。

 相關句子Related Wordings

Track 60

☑ What faculty were you in?

你的專業是什麼？

☑ During the probation period your salary will be 82 thousand per month, is it acceptable for you?

在試用期間您的薪水是8萬2千，這樣可以接受嗎？

☑ What will happen after the probation period?

試用期之後會怎麼樣？

☑ This is a fare company.

這間公司福利真好。

☑ How much holiday time am I allowed?

我可以放幾天年假？

☑ What do you do?

你的職務是什麼？

Track 61

☑ Will I have medical insurance and year evaluation?

我會有健保跟年終嗎？

☑ Today is my first day at my new job.

今天是我新工作的第一天。

☑ What should I wear today?

我應該穿什麼呢？

☑ What is the nature of your call?

請問您打電話來有什麼事？

☑ I wish to make a complaint.

我想要客訴。

☑ I would like to apply for some holiday time.

我想要申請一些假期。

I am English
Coversation King

休閒旅遊

Travel

➲ 旅遊

A What do you plan to do during this tour?

這趟旅遊你有什麼計畫？

B I want to go shopping, and go to Mt. Alps. And you?

我想去逛街，然後去阿爾卑斯山。你呢？

A I want to go on to the Eiffel Tower and have nice meals.

我想要去艾菲爾鐵塔，享受美食。

B Sounds nice.

聽起來不錯。

A Where do you want to go shopping?

你想要去哪裡逛街？

B I have no idea, I wish to buy some beautiful, nice quality, not too expensive clothes. Especially European style.

我也不知道。我想要買漂亮,有質感的,不要太貴的衣服。特別是歐洲風格的。

A I think we have to ask Kate for some advice.

我覺得我們應該問一下凱特,請她給我們一些建議。

B You are right.

說得對。

A Do you have Kate's phone?

你有凱特的電話嗎?

B Yes. I'll call her.

有。我打給她。

我是**英語會話王**
I am English Coversation King

Track 63

Hotel reservation

➲ 飯店訂房

A I would like to make a reservation.

我想訂房。

B May I have your full name?

可以給我您的全名嗎？

A Jane Taylor.

珍 泰勒。

B Your phone number?

您的電話？

A 1234567.

1234567.

Track 63

B Do you want a single or a double room?
您要單人房或者雙人房？

A Single room, please.
單人房謝謝。

B On which date will you be coming in?
請問入住的日期是哪一天？

A Sep. 23.
九月23日。

B How many days are you staying?
請問要停留幾天？

A 1 week. Will I have a view of the sea?
一個禮拜。我可以看到海景嗎？

B Yes, I will arrange you with a good view room.
可以，我會為您安排有美景的房間。

我是**英語會話王**
I am English Coversation King

A Can I pay it by cash, then?

我可以用現金付費嗎？

B Sure.

當然。

A How much will it be?

這樣要多少錢？

B It will be 700 dollars for 7 days.

七天的話是美金700元。

A Is breakfast included?

有包含早餐嗎？

B Yes, breakfast is included.

有，有包含早餐。

At the Check in counter in Airport

➲ 在機場的櫃台

A Can I see your ticket and passport?

我可以看您的護照嗎？

A How many suitcases are you going to check in?

您要拖運幾件行李？

B One.

一件。

A Do you have any electronics?

有任何電子產品嗎？

B Yes, my hand phone is here.

有，我的手機在這兒。

A Ok, make sure there is no lighter or battery in the suitcase.

好，請確定您託運的行李廂中沒有打火機或者電池。

B Oh, my power bank is in the suitcase. Is that OK?

噢，我的行動電源在行李箱裡面。這樣可以嗎？

A I'm afraid that you have to take it out with you in your handbag.

恐怕要請您將它拿出來在在手提包中隨身攜帶了。

A Also, water, knife will not be allowed to bring up to the plane with you.

還有，水和刀子都不能隨身攜帶上飛機。

A Do you like a window or aisle seat?

■ 請問要靠窗或是走道？

B Window, please.
靠窗，謝謝。

B What is the boarding time?
登機時間是何時？

A 10:35. It is shown here. And your departure gate is A7.

10:35。寫在這邊。您的登機口是A7

B Thank you.
謝謝。

A Have a nice trip.

祝旅途愉快。

At the customs 1

⊃ 通關1

A Could I see your passport?

我可以看你的護照嗎？

B Yes, here it is.

可以，在這邊。

A And the plane ticket, please.

還有機票，謝謝。

B Here.

在這裡。

A Where will you be staying?

你會住在哪邊？

B At the Hyatt Hotel.

希爾頓飯店。

A Where is the hotel?

飯店在哪裡？

B New York.

紐約。

A How long will you be staying?

你會停留多久？

B For 1 month.

一個月。

A Do you have anything to declair?

你有東西要申報的嗎？

B No.

沒有。

A Put your fingers on the machine and look at the camera here.

把你的手指放在機器上，看這邊的鏡頭。

B Yes.
好的。

A Have a nice vacation.
祝旅途愉快。

B Thank you.
謝謝。

At the customs 2

➲ 通關2

A May I see your passport, please?

我可以看您的護照嗎？

B Yes.

好。

A And your immigration card?

您的簽證呢？

B Yes, here you are.

有，在這邊。

A Do you have anything to declare?

有東西要申報的嗎？

B No.

沒有。

我是**英語會話王**
I am English Coversation King

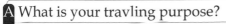

A What is your travling purpose?

您來訪的目的是什麼？

B Visiting.

觀光。

A How long will you be staying in USA?

你會停留在美國多久？

B 2 weeks.

2週。

A Where will you be staying?

你會停留在哪裡？

B I will be in New York and L.A.

我會在紐約和洛杉磯。

A Which Hotel?

哪間飯店？

B I will stay in my friend's house in New York, and stay in the Beverly Hills Hotel in LA.

我會住在紐約的朋友家裡，和洛杉磯的比佛利山莊酒店。

A Have you got any food with you?

你身上有帶食物嗎？

B No. I haven't got any food with me.

沒有，我身上沒有帶食物。

A Welcome to USA.

歡迎來美國。

我是**英語會話王**
I am English Coversation King

In the airport

⊃ 在機場

A Excuse me. Where can I find my suitcase.

請問一下。我要去哪裡找我的行李箱？

B What flight were you on?

您搭哪一班飛機？

B Your suitcase will come out from the H baggage carousel.

您的行李會從H出來。

A Could it be possible that someone else took it away?

有可能被別人拿走嗎？

B Do you have a name on your suitcase?

您有標示您的名字嗎？

A Yes, I wrote it on the label.

有，我有寫在標牌上。

B Let me see your passport, please.

請讓我看一下你的護照。

A Here it is.

在這裡。

B Sir, your case might be taken to that counter.

先生，您的行李廂有可能被拿到那個櫃台了。

A Ok, thank you.

好的，謝謝。

我是**英語會話王**
I am English Coversation King

Track 68

Information desk

➲ 詢問台

A I'm going to New York, how can I go there?

我想要去紐約，要怎麼過去呢？

B You may take the subway or bus.

您可以搭地鐵或者巴士。

A Where do I take the bus?

要在哪邊搭巴士？

B It is outside of this building and you could buy the ticket there.

在這棟建築物外面，票可以在那邊買。

at the Hotel Reception desk

➲ 在飯店櫃檯

A I'd like to check in, please.

我想辦理入住。

B Do you have a reservation?

有訂房嗎？

A Yes, it is in the name of JJ.

有，名字是JJ。

B Here is your key.

這是您的鑰匙。

B The room is on the 7th floor.

您的房間在7樓。

我是**英語會話王**
I am English Coversation King

A Do I have a view to the sea from this room?

我的房間可以看到海嗎？

B Yes, you have an excellent view to the sea from this room.

可以，從您的房間可以看到非常美麗的海景。

A Thanks.

謝謝。

A Where can I get something to eat?

哪裡有吃的呢？

B There are some resturants on B1 floor and there is a café on the 2 floor, also.

B1有餐廳，2樓也有咖啡廳。

A What time is breakfast served in the morning?

早餐供應的時間是幾點？

B It is served from 6 to 10.

從6點到10點。

A Is there anything interesting near this area?

這個區域有什麼有趣的東西嗎？

B There will be a musical show, Notre Dame de Paris.

有一齣音樂劇鐘樓怪人的表演。

A Is it performed in French?

用法語演出？

B Yeah, I guess.

是啊，我想應該是吧。

Dinning in hotel

➲ 在飯店用餐

A Are you dining alone?

您一個人用餐嗎？

B Yes.

是。

A Smoking?

抽菸嗎？

B Non-smoking.

不抽菸。

A This way. Here is the menu, I will come back later to take your order.

這邊。這是菜單，我等一下回來為您點餐。

B Can I pay by credit card?

■ 我可以用信用卡付費嗎？

A Yes, we take VISA cards.

可以，我們接受VISA卡。

B OK. I see.

好。我知道了。

B OK. I see. By the way, would you bring me a glass of water?

好。我知道了。喔對了，你可以給我一杯水嗎？

A Yes. Please wait a moment.

好的。請稍等。

 相關句子Related Wordings

Track 71

☑ I would like to have a morning call at 8:00 in the morning.

早上8：00請打電話叫醒我。

我是**英語會話王**
I am English Coversation King

☑ I'd like to order room service, please.

我要食物送到房間的服務。

☑ I'd like a single room.

我要單人房。

☑ I'd like a twin room.

我要兩張床的房間。

☑ I'd like as extra bed for room 702.

我要在702房多加一張床。

☑ When is check out time?

退房的適合時間？

☑ I'd like to book a room.

我想訂房。

☑ How much is a double room for 1 night?

雙人床一晚多少呢？

☑ Your booking is confirmed.

Track 72

你的訂房已經生效了。

☑ Do you have a bus service from the airport?

有機場接送巴士嗎？

☑ Could you show me my room?

你可以帶我到我的房間嗎？

☑ Where is the emergency exit and staircase?

緊急出口和樓梯在那裏？

☑ Please send another blanket to my room.

請再送一條毯子到我房間。

☑ Please bring me some ice cubes and water.

請送給我一些冰塊和水。

☑ The sheets are dirty.

床單很髒。

☑ There's no running hot water in my room.

我房間沒有熱水。

☑ I'll arrive late, but please keep my reservation.

我會晚一點到達，請保留所預訂的房間。

☑ I'd like a room with a nice view.

我想要一間視野好的房間。

☑ What time does the dining room open?

餐廳幾點開始營業？

☑ What time can I have breakfast?

早餐幾點開始供應？

☑ Could you keep my valuables?

是否可代為保管貴重物品？

☑ I'd like to check out. My bill, please.

我要退房。請給我帳單。

☑ The air-conditioner doesn't work.

冷氣壞了。

Chatting2

⊃ 聊天2

A I need to take some exercise.

我需要運動。

B So do I, I am getting on weight these days.

我也是，我最近一直變胖。

A I'd like to take a walk around.

我想要在附近散散步。

B Why don't we ride the bicycles along the river nearby?

我們何不沿著河畔騎腳踏車？

A So romantic.

好浪漫喔。

B Does that means OK?

■ 這是好的意思嗎？

A Yes, sure.
是啊，對。

B I like your smile.
我喜歡你的笑容。

A I like your humor.
我喜歡你的幽默。

Grand Canyon National Park

➲ 大峽谷國家公園

A So huge!

好巨大！

B Incredible!

太強了！

A It is so great!

好偉大！

B So big!

真大！

A Astonishing!

令人驚嘆！

B God is so great.
神好偉大。

A I feel so small in front of nature.

在大自然面前我感到自己好渺小。

B Yeah, human is so small.
是啊，人類很渺小。

A Sometimes we stuck in too small things and worry too much.

有時候我們陷入在太小的事情了，也擔心太多事了。

B You are right. I want to throw away all my worries down there!
沒錯。我想要把我的煩惱通通丟下去！

A I want to jump to the opposite.

我想要跳到對面去。

B Be careful!

■ 小心！

A I did it!

我成功了！

B It was close! So dangerous!

好險唉！危險啊！

A Thank God I'm alive.

感謝神我活著。

B Thank God you are alive.

感謝神你活著。

A I was told that there will be star party in the night here, it is very beautiful.

我聽説這邊晚上會有賞星派對，很美喔。

B Do you mean the star night?

你是説夜晚的星空嗎？

A Yes, let's come later in the night.

是啊，我們晚上再來吧。

B I can't wait!

我迫不及待！

B OK. Let's go have dinner.

好。我們去吃晚餐。

A Why don't we take some pictures before we go?

我們要不要先拍照再走？

B Good idea.

好主意。

A We can enjoy the starry sky. If lucky, we can even see the Milkyway.

我們可以欣賞星空。夠幸運的話，甚至可以看到銀河喔。

Stonehenge 1

➔ 巨石陣

A I can't wait to go to the Stonehenge!

我等不及要去巨石陣了！

B Did you find out how to go there?

你有找到去那裡的方法了嗎？

A Yeah. I've surfed the internet and got this, Scarper Tours.

有。我搜尋了網路，找到這個，Scarper Tours。

B How can we buy the tickets?

我們要怎麼買票？

A It says we can just book on the site and show them the confirmation email then we can take the bus.

他說只要上網訂位，到時候秀給他們看訂位確認

■ 的信就可以搭上巴士了。

B How do we pay?
要怎麼付錢？

A Pay when we get on the bus.
上巴士的時候付就可以。

B Did you got the confirmation email?
有收到確認信了嗎？

A Let me see. Yes, I got it.
我看一下。 有，收到了。

B So let's go print it out.
那我們去印出來吧。

A Oh, we don't have to. We just show them this email on my mobile phone and everything is OK.

喔，不必列印啊，到時候我的手機秀出這封信就好囉。

B Wow. It is convenient.
哇。好方便喔。

A Let's go!
我們走吧！

B Now?
現在?

A I mean let's go for lunch!
我是說我們去吃午餐吧！

我是**英語會話王**
I am English Coversation King

Stonehenge 2
➲ 巨石陣2

A I love the grasslands.

我喜歡這片草地。

B Green is good for your eyes.
綠色對眼睛很好。

A I feel so relaxed and excited.

我覺得好放鬆又興奮喔。

B Thank God it's a sunny day.
感謝上天，天氣很好。

A Thank God.

感謝神。

B See the stones!
你看這些岩石！

A They are so big!

好大喔！

B I can feel the magical power.

我可以感受到一股神祕的氣息。

A So amazing.

好神奇喔。

B It is a clock in ancient times?

這是不是古代的時鐘啊？

A I don't know.

我不知道。

Cambridge
➲ 劍橋

A Have you been to Cambridge yet?

你有去過劍橋嗎？

B Not yet.

還沒。

A It's worth visiting, I suggest you go punting on the River Cam.

很值得去參觀喔，我建議你去康河坐撐篙船。

B What is punting?

撐篙是什麼？

A It is a kind of boat. People take the boat and sightseeing the Cambridge on the river. Let me show you some pictures.

那是一種船。 大家會坐船在河上參觀劍橋大學。
我查一下照片給你看。

B Wow~that's wonderful!
哇~~好棒喔！

A You want to go?
想去嗎？

B Yes! Take me there.
想！帶我去。

A Sure!
當然！

B Wait, do we have to do punting by our-
selves?
等一下，我們要自己撐篙嗎？

A No, don't worry.
不用，別擔心。

Covent Garden

➲ 柯芬園

A Martin, would you tell me where I can buy gifts for my family?

馬汀，你可以告訴我我該在哪裡買禮物給我家人嗎？

B Mmm, I think Covent Garden is the best choice.

嗯，我覺得柯芬園是最棒的選擇。

A Where is it?

那在哪裡？

B It's in London. We just have to take the Tube.

在倫敦啊。搭地鐵就可以到喔。

A Great. You are really a perfect guide.

■ 讚。你真的是完美的嚮導。

B I can even tell you the stories about the garden later.

我等一下還可以告訴你有關那裡的故事唷。

A I'll be looking forward to it.

我會好好期待的。

B I guess you won't mind if they are ghost stories?

我想你應不會介意那是鬼故事吧？

A Oh, I do mind. Please don't tell me.

噢，我介意。請不要跟我說。

 相關句子Related Wordings

Track 79

☑ I would like to make a reservation.

我想預約。

我是**英語會話王**
I am English Coversation King

☑ How many days do you plan to stay?

預計要停留幾天？

☑ I will stay for 7 days.

我預計要待7天。

☑ Which room type do you want?

您要哪種房間？

☑ Single room, please.

請給我單人房。

☑ Twin room, please.

請給我兩張單人床的房間。

☑ Double room, please.

請給我一張雙人床的房間。

☑ How much does it cost for one night?

一天晚上要多少？

☑ It is 100 dollars per night.

一天晚上100元。

☑ When will you come?

你什麼時候來？

☑ Jan. 23.

一月23日。

☑ When can I check in?

我幾點可以入住？

☑ When should I check out?

我最晚幾點必須退房？

Get lost

➲ 迷路

A I'm lost.

我迷路了。

B Where are you going?

你想去哪裡？

A I wan to go to Jardin des Tuileries Garden.

我想杜樂麗花園。

B I don't know that place, sorry.

我不知道那個地方，抱歉。

A Do you know where the public telephone is?

你知道公共電話在哪裡嗎？

B It is over there.
在那邊。

A Hello, Martin. I am lost.
喂，馬汀。我迷路了。

C Where are you?
你在哪裡？

A I am in front of Café de Flore.
我在花神咖啡廳前面。

C Stay there, wait for me. I'm coming to you.
待在那邊，等我。我去找你。

我是**英語會話王**
I am English Coversation King

Changing the flight

➲ 換班機時間

A I want to change my departure day, please.

我想要換班機日期。

B Can I have your name, please?
請給我您的名字。

A My name is Ken Lopez.

我的名字是肯‧羅茲。

B Which day would you like to change to?
您想要改到哪一天？

A I would like to change to Nov. 23rd afternoon.

■ 我想要改到11月23日下午。

B Let me check. Yes, it is possible. So I will change your departure day to Nov.23rd on 4:35PM, the flight NO. is BTG888. Will that be fine?

讓我確認一下。有，可以的。那我為您變更班機時間到11月23日下午4點35分，班機號碼是BTG888。這樣可以嗎？

A Yes, good. Thank you.

可以的，很好。謝謝您。

B You are welcome.

不客氣。

相關句子Related Wordings

Track 82

☑ Where am I?

我在哪裡？

☑ Where is the nearest bus station?

我是**英語會話王**
I am English Coversation King

最近的巴士站在哪？

☑ How can I get to London bridge?

要怎麼去倫敦橋？

☑ When is the last train?

最後一班車是幾點？

單字補充

Café
咖啡廳

Cafeteria	咖啡廳
Caramel Macchiato	焦糖瑪奇朵
Caffe Americano	美式
Caffe Mocha	摩卡
Caffe Latte	拿鐵
Cappuccino	卡布奇諾
Iced Caffe Latte	冰拿鐵
Iced Caffe Mocha	冰摩卡
Iced Caffe Americano	冰美式
Mango Citrus Tea Frappuccino	芒果茶星冰樂
Caramel Cream Frappuccino	焦糖星冰樂
Vanilla Cream Frappuccino	香草星冰樂

Track 84

Track 84

Chocolate Cream Frappuccino	巧克力星冰樂
Muffin	馬芬蛋糕
Classic Chocolate Cake	法式巧克力蛋糕
Black Forest Cake	黑森林蛋糕
Cheese Cake	起司蛋糕
Blueberry Cheese Cake	藍莓起司蛋糕
Pizza	比薩

我是**英語會話王**
I am English Coversation King

Vegetable & Ham Pie
蔬菜火腿派

Cookies	餅乾
Tiramisu	提拉米蘇
Sandwich	三明治
black tea	紅茶
green tea	綠茶
jasmine tea	茉莉花茶
juice	果汁
orange juice	柳橙汁
apple juice	蘋果汁
grape juice	葡萄汁
Green Tea Latte	抹茶拿鐵
Earl Grey	伯爵紅茶
Iced Rose Fancy Tea Latte	冰玫瑰蜜香茶那堤

Track 84

Iced Green Tea Latte	冰抹茶那堤
Tea Misto	茶密斯朵
Oriental Beauty Oolong Tea	東方美人
Iced Black Tea Latte	冰經典紅茶那堤
Iced Shaken Lemon Tea	冰搖檸檬茶

Car
汽車

BENZ	賓士
BMW	BMW
Citroen	雪鐵龍
Ferrari	法拉利
AUDI	奧迪
FORD	福特
HUNDAI	現代
VOLVO	富豪
OPEL	歐普
PEUGEOT	寶獅
PORSCHE	保時捷
RENAULT	雷諾
SAAB	紳寶
LEXUS	凌志

BENTLEY	賓特利
Lamborghini	藍寶堅尼
Cadillac	凱迪拉克
MITSUBISHI	三菱
Ford	福特
Audi	奧迪
Honda	本田
Toyota	豐田
Nissan	日產
VOLVO	富豪

Stationary
文具

pen	原子筆
pencil	鉛筆
mechanical pencil	自動鉛筆
highlighter	螢光筆
pencil cup	筆筒
eraser	橡皮擦
notebook	筆記本
glue	膠水
ruler	尺
stapler	釘書機
staple	釘書針
correction tap	修正帶
knife	小刀
scissors	剪刀

post-It note	便條紙
envelopes	信封
paper clips	迴紋針
calculator	計算機
paper	影印紙
pen	原子筆
pencil	鉛筆
pencil cup	筆筒
magnet	磁鐵

我是**英語會話王**
I am English Coversation King

Free Time Activities
休閒活動

cycling	騎腳踏車
attend classes	上課
surf the Internet	上網
visit a park	公園
go for a walk	散步
go out for a drink	喝杯飲料
go out for dinner	出門吃晚餐
go shopping	逛街
go to the beach	去海邊
go out with friends	跟朋友出去
exercise	運動
play a sport	球類運動
play a musical instrument	玩樂器
cook	料理，煮菜

gardening	園藝
listen to music	聽音樂
hiking	健行
tour	旅遊
worship	禮拜
visit friends	找朋友
volleyball	排球
watch a movie	看電影
watch a performance	看表演
watch TV	看電視
writing	寫作

Sports
運動

Basketball	籃球
Volleyball	排球
Dodge Ball	躲避球
Ping-Pong Ball	乒乓球
soccer	足球
American football	美式足球
baseball	棒球
badminton	羽毛球
tennis	網球
handball	手球
softball	壘球
water polo	水球
cricket	板球
hockey	曲棍球

ice hockey	冰上曲棍球
billiards	撞球
bowling	保齡球
swimming	游泳
cycling	自行車
running	跑步
beach volleyball	沙灘排球
baseball	棒球
tennis	網球

Color
顏色

red	紅
pink	粉紅
baby pink	淺粉紅
orange	橙
yellow	黃
green	綠
blue	藍
sky blue	天藍
royal blue	寶藍
navy	靛色
purple	紫
white	白
milk white	乳白
ivory	象牙白

gold	金色
silver	銀色
transparent	透明
translucent	半透明
rose golden	玫瑰金
light yellow	鵝黃
mustard	芥末黃
khaki	卡其
olive green	橄欖綠
sky blue	蔚藍
baby blue	淺藍

Clothes
衣服

coat	外套、大衣
one-piece	洋裝，連身裙
jacket	短外套
coat	長外套
demin	牛仔褲
pyjama	睡衣
apparel	正裝
blouse	女襯衫
suit	套裝/西裝
shirt	襯衫
business suit	西裝
trousers	褲子(總稱)
short pants	短褲
jeans	牛仔褲

sport pants	運動褲
evening gown	晚禮服
football shirt	足球衫
hooded shirt	連帽 T
hoodie	連帽T恤
leather jacket	皮衣
short pants	短褲
swimming trunks	海灘褲
swimsuit	游泳裝

Shoes
鞋子

high-heels	高跟鞋
sneakers	球鞋
sandals	涼鞋
slippers	拖鞋
casual shoes	休閒鞋
leather shoe	皮鞋
boots	靴子
canvas shoes	帆布鞋
casual shoes	休閒鞋
high-top sneakers	籃球鞋
heelless shoes	平底女鞋

Beverage
飲料

black tea	紅茶
green tea	綠茶
iced tea	冰紅茶
oolong tea	烏龍茶
bubble tea	珍珠奶茶
apple juice	蘋果汁
grape juice	葡萄汁
lemonade	檸檬汁
coconut juice	椰子汁

Fruit
水果

apple	蘋果
orange	橘子
banana	香蕉
melon	哈密瓜
blueberry	藍莓
lemon	檸檬
mango	芒果
watermelon	西瓜
strawberry	草莓
honey peach	水蜜桃
pear	梨子
cherry	櫻桃
durian	榴槤
coconut	椰子

cranberry	蔓越橘，小紅莓
citron	柚子
kiwi	奇異果
lemon	檸檬
mango	芒果
blueberry	藍莓
carambola	楊桃
jambu air	蓮霧
loquat	枇杷
papaya	木瓜
passion fruit	百香果

Vegetable
蔬菜

carrot	紅蘿蔔
taro	芋頭
olive	橄欖
sweet potato	地瓜
tomato	番茄
asparagus	蘆筍
broccoli	花椰菜
potato	馬鈴薯
potato	馬鈴薯
spinach	菠菜
needle mushroom	金針菇
garlic	蒜頭
ginger	薑
chilli	辣椒

Chinese chives	韭菜
green onion	蔥
Chinese parsley	香菜
green pepper	青椒
soybean sprout	黃豆芽
cucumber	黃瓜
eggplant	茄子
pumpkin	南瓜
aloe	蘆薈
cabbage	高麗菜
carrot	紅蘿蔔
mushrooms	洋菇
yam	山藥

Track 95

Movement
各種動作

stand	站
sit	坐
lie	躺
stretch and yawn	伸懶腰
sneeze	打噴嚏
yawn	打哈欠
hiccup	打嗝
snore	打鼾
cough	咳嗽

Body
身體

eye	眼睛
month	嘴巴
nose	鼻子
ear	耳朵
hand	手
leg	腿
foot	腳
hair	頭髮

Steak
牛排

Rare	一分熟
Medium Rare	三分熟
Medium	五分熟
Medium Well	七分熟
Well Done	全熟

animal
動物

bird	鳥
eagle	老鷹
pigeon	鴿子
dove	鴿子
turtle	烏龜
crow	烏鴉
owl	貓頭鷹
gull	海鷗
sparrow	麻雀
dog	狗
cat	貓
cattle	牛
cow	母牛
ox	公牛

tiger	虎
rabbit	兔
dragon	龍
snake	蛇
horse	馬
goat	山羊
sheep	綿羊
lamb	小羊
monkey	猴子
chicken	雞
rooster	公雞
hen	母雞
pig	豬
rabbit	兔
tiger	虎
lion	獅子

dragon	龍
elephant	大象
leopard	豹
deer	鹿
antelope	羚羊
wolf	狼
donkey	驢子
squirrel	松鼠
mouse	鼠
bear	熊
polar bear	北極熊
penguin	企鵝
dolphin	海豚
sharks	鯊魚
jellyfish	水母
fish	魚

Number
數字

one	1
two	2
three	3
four	4
five	5
six	6
seven	7
eight	8
nine	9
ten	10
hundred	百
thousand	千
ten thousand	萬
hundred thousand	10萬

million	百萬
ten million	千萬
hundred million	億
billion	十億
ten billion	百億
hundred billion	千億

I am English
Coversation King

生活常用句

Daily English Sentences

➲ 生活常用句

☑ Hi.

嗨。

☑ Hello.

哈囉。

☑ How are you?

你好嗎？

☑ How is everything?

一切都好嗎？

☑ How do you do?

初次見面。

☑ Nice to meet you.

很高興認識你。

☑ Yes.
是。

Track 101

☑ No.
不是。

☑ Pardon?
什麼？(請再說一次)

☑ OK.
好。

☑ How's everything?
一切都好嗎？

☑ Great!
很好！

☑ Thank you.
謝謝。

我是**英語會話王**
I am English Coversation King

☑ Thank you very much.
非常謝謝。

☑ You're welcome.
不客氣。

☑ My pleasure.
這是我的榮幸。

☑ I see.
我明白了。

☑ I know.
我知道。

☑ Good job!
做得好！

☑ Congratulations!
恭喜！

☑ Sorry.
抱歉。

☑ Excuse me.
不好意思。

☑ I don't know.
我不知道。

Track 102

☑ Are you alright?
你還好嗎?

☑ Would you like one?
你要不要一個?

☑ Can I help you?
需要幫忙嗎?

☑ Long time no see.
好久不見。

☑ My treat.
我請客。

☑ Count me in.
算我一份,我要參加。

我是**英語會話王**
I am English Coversation King

☑ I agree.
我同意。

☑ God bless you.
願神保守你。

☑ Keep in touch.
保持聯絡。

☑ I like it.
我喜歡。

☑ Me, too.
我也是。

☑ Have a nice day.
祝你有美好的一天。

☑ You, too.
你也是。

☑ My God!
天啊！

☑ You are so beautiful!
  妳真美！

☑ Wait!
  等一下！

Track 103

☑ Watch out!
  小心！

☑ Stop!
  停！

☑ Enough.
  夠了。

☑ Don't move!
  不許動！

☑ Time's up.
  時間到。

☑ Have fun!
  玩得開心！

我是**英語會話王**
I am English Coversation King

Track 103

☑ I'm lost.
我迷路了。

☑ Don't worry.
別擔心。

☑ I love you!
我愛你！

☑ I'm hungry.
好餓。

☑ Is this yours?
這是你的嗎？

☑ As soon as possible!
越快越好！

☑ May I use your pen?
我可以用你的筆嗎？

☑ How much is it?
多少錢？

Chapter7
生活常用句

☑ Goodbye.
再見。

☑ See you.
再見。

Track 104

☑ See you soon.
再見。

☑ See you next time.
下次見。

☑ See you tomorrow.
明天見。

☑ Good evening.
晚安。（大約5~8點）

☑ Good night.
晚安。（大約9點之後）

☑ Please.
請。拜託。

我是**英語會話王**
I am English Coversation King

☑ I'll do it.
我來做。

☑ Really?
真的嗎？

☑ Please come in.
請進。

☑ Please follow me.
請跟我來。

☑ What kind of persons do you like?
你喜歡哪種人？

☑ How did you do on the test?
考得怎麼樣？

☑ How have you been in Europe?
在歐洲過得如何？

☑ How kind of you!
你人真好！

☑ How thoughtful of you!
你好體貼喔！

☑ How smart of you!
你好聰明喔！

Track 105

☑ How sweet of you!
你好貼心喔！

☑ Please introduce yourself.
請你自我介紹一下。

☑ It is our anniversary today.
今天是我們的紀念日。

☑ Why don't we go shopping after school?
我們下課後要不要去逛街？

☑ Why don't we take the stairs?
我們要不要走樓梯？

☑ Why don't we take a walk together after work?

我是**英語會話王**
I am English Conversation King

我們下班後要不要散散步？

☑ Why don't we go to the beach this weekend?
我們這個週末去海邊如何？

☑ Good idea.
好主意。

☑ Absolutely!
沒錯！

☑ After you.
您先。

☑ Allow me.
讓我來。

☑ Amazing!
驚人的好！

☑ Any day will do.
哪一天都行。

☑ Any messages for me?
有我的留言嗎？

☑ Anything else?
還要別的嗎？

Track 106

☑ Anybody home?
有人在家嗎？

☑ Are you kidding?
你在開玩笑吧。

☑ Are you married or single?
你結婚了嗎？

☑ Are you OK?
你還好嗎？

☑ Are you okay?
你還好嗎？

☑ Are you sure?
你肯定嗎？

我是**英語會話王**
I am English Coversation King

☑ As soon as possible.
越快越好。

☑ At last.
終於。

☑ Attention, please.
請注意。

☑ Awesome!
太讚了！

☑ Be my guest.
請接受我的邀請。／ 請便！

☑ Be quiet.
安靜點。

☑ Beautiful!
漂亮！水！

☑ Believe it or not.
信不信由你。

☑ Better late than never.
遲了也是比不去做還要更好。

☑ Bless you.
祝福你。

Track 107

☑ Bon appetit.
祝用餐愉快。

☑ Bon voyage.
一路平安。

☑ Call me.
打電話給我。

☑ Call the police!
叫警察！

☑ Calm down.
冷靜。

☑ Can I get a ride?
我可以搭便車嗎？

我是**英語會話王**
I am English Coversation King

☑ Can you describe yourself?

你可以描述一下自己嗎？

☑ Certainly.

當然。

☑ Check it out.

看一下。／查看一下。／確認一下。

☑ Cheer up.

振作起來。

☑ Clothes make the man.

人要衣裝。

☑ Come here.

過來。

☑ Come in, please.

請進！

☑ Come on!

來吧！／趕快！

Track 108

☑ Congratulations!

恭喜！

☑ Control yourself.

克制一下。

☑ Definitely.

肯定是。

☑ Did you get it?

你有理解嗎？

☑ Did you miss the bus?

你錯過公車了？

☑ Do l have to?

非做不可嗎？

☑ Do you speak English?

你會說英語嗎？

☑ Do you speak Mandarin?

你會說中文嗎？

我是**英語會話王**
I am English Coversation King

☑ Does he like ice-cream?
他喜歡吃冰淇淋嗎？

☑ Don't give up.
別放棄。

☑ Don't go.
別走。

☑ Don't be so childish.
別這麼孩子氣。

☑ Don't fall for it.
別上當。

☑ Don't give me that.
少來這套。

☑ Don't let me down.
別讓我失望。

☑ Don't lose your head.
不要慌。

☑ Don't move.
不許動。

☑ Don't trust to chance.
不要碰運氣。

☑ Don't worry.
別擔心。

☑ East, west, home is best.
金窩銀窩，不如自己的狗窩。

☑ lovely day, isn't it?
好天氣，是不是啊？

☑ Enjoy yourself.
祝你玩得開心。

☑ Excellent!
非常好！

☑ Excuse me, Sir.
不好意思，先生。

☑ Excuse me.

不好意思。/ 借過。

☑ Excuse me...

請問…

☑ Excuse me?

請再說一遍好嗎？

☑ Fantastic!

夢幻般美好！

☑ Far from it.

差得遠呢。 / 才不是。

☑ 30 divided by 5 equals 6.

30除以5等於6。

☑ Fasten your seat belt.

安全帶繫好。

☑ Feel better?

好點了嗎？

☑ Fire!
火啊！

☑ First come first served.
先到先贏。

☑ Follow me.
跟我來。

☑ Forget it.
休想！/ 算了。

☑ Get out of my way.
閃開。

☑ Give me a hand.
幫我一下。

☑ Go for it.
試試看吧！

☑ God bless you.
願神保守你。

☑ Good afternoon.
午安。

☑ Good evening.
晚安。

☑ Good idea.
好主意。

☑ Good job.
做得好。

☑ Good luck.
祝你好運。

☑ Good luck.
祝好運。

☑ Good morning.
早安。

☑ Good night
晚安。

☑ Goodbye.
再見。

☑ Great minds think alike.
英雄所見略同。

☑ Great!
很好！

☑ Guess what?
你猜怎麼了。

☑ Have fun.
玩得開心。

☑ He always talks big.
他總是吹牛。

☑ He can hardly speak.
他幾乎說不出話來。

☑ He can't take a joke.
他開不得玩笑。

☑ He grasped my hands.
他緊握住我的手。

☑ He has a large income.
他有很高的收入。

☑ He has a sense of humor.
他有幽默感。

☑ He is collecting money.
他在籌集資金。

☑ He is fed up with his work.
他對工作煩死了。

☑ He is looking for a job.
他正在找工作。

☑ He is my age.
他和我同年。

☑ He looks very healthy.
他看來很健康。

☑ He owes me \$30.
他欠我30美元。

☑ He repaired his car.
他修理了他的車。

☑ He suggested a picnic.
他建議辦野餐。

☑ He was born in New York.
他出生在紐約。

☑ He was not a bit tired.
他一點也不累。

☑ He won an election.
他在選舉中獲勝。

☑ Help yourself.
別客氣。

☑ Help!
救命啊！

我是**英語會話王**
I am English Coversation King

☑ Here you are.
給你。

☑ Here's a gift for you.
這個禮物送給你。

☑ Hold on.
等一下。

☑ How about you?
你呢？

☑ How come?
怎麼會（這樣）？

☑ How do I look?
我看起來怎麼樣？

☑ How is it going?
一切可好？

☑ How much does it cost?
多少錢？

☑ How much is this?
這個多少錢？

☑ How much?
多少錢？

☑ How old are you?
你幾歲？

☑ How's everything?
最近如何？

☑ How's it going?
怎麼樣？

☑ I agree.
我同意。

☑ I am coming.
我來了。

☑ I am impressed.
令我印象深刻。

☑ I am so sorry.
我非常抱歉。

☑ I am touched.
我好感動。

☑ I can barely hear you.
我幾乎聽不到你說的。

☑ I can tell.
我看得出來。

☑ I can't stand it.
我無法忍受。

☑ I can't afford it.
我買不起。/ 我承當不起。

☑ I can't follow you.
我不懂你說的。

☑ I can't hear you very well.
我聽不太清楚。

☑ I can't help it.
　我情不自禁。

☑ I can't stop sneezing.
　我打噴嚏打個不停。

☑ I care about you.
　我在乎你。

☑ I caught the last train of Taipei Metro.
　我趕上了最後一班捷運。

☑ I could hardly speak.
　我簡直說不出話來。

☑ I decline.
　我拒絕。

☑ I develop films myself.
　我自己沖洗照片。

☑ I didn't catch you.
　對不起，我沒聽懂你說的。

☑ I don't care.
不關我的事 / 我不管。

☑ I don't know for sure.
我不確切知道。

☑ I don't know.
我不知道。

☑ I don't mean it.
我不是故意的。

☑ I don't think so.
我不這麼想。

☑ I don't understand.
我聽不懂。

☑ I doubt it.
我懷疑。

☑ I enjoyed a lot.
我玩得很開心。

☑ I felt no regret for it.
對這件事我不覺得後悔。

☑ I felt sort of ill.
我感覺有點不適。

☑ I get up at seven o'clock.
我7點起床。

☑ I got it!
我懂了！

☑ I got to go.
我該走了。

☑ I guess so.
我想是吧。

☑ I have a good idea.
我有一個好主意。

☑ I have a stuffy nose.
我鼻塞。

☑ I have no choice.
我別無選擇。

☑ I have no idea.
我沒有頭緒。

☑ I have the right to know.
我有權知道。

☑ I heard someone laughing.
我聽見有人在笑。

☑ I know all about it.
我知道有關它的一切。

☑ I like it.
我喜歡。

☑ I like your style.
我喜歡你的風格。

☑ I love you with all my heart
我全心全意愛你！

Track 116

☑ I love you.
我愛你。

☑ I mean it.
我是認真的。

☑ I met him.
我見到他了。

☑ I miss you.
我想你。

☑ I must get going.
我得走了。

☑ I owe you.
我欠你。

☑ I promise.
我保證。

☑ I quit.
我不幹了。

我是**英語會話王**
I am English Coversation King

☑ I see.
　我明白了。

☑ I suppose so.
　我想是吧。

☑ I think so.
　我也這麼想。

☑ I understand.
　我聽得懂。

☑ I walked across the squre.
　我穿越廣場。

☑ I want to reserve a table for five.
　我想預約五個人的座位。

☑ I want to reserve a table.
　我想預約位置。

☑ I want to see you now.
　我現在就想見到你。

☑ I want to wash my car this weekend.
我這週末想要洗車。

☑ I will be more careful.
我會小心一些的。

☑ I will miss you.
我會想你的。

☑ I will never forget it.
我不會忘記的。

☑ I wish you were here.
真希望你在這裡。

☑ I'm in love!
我戀愛了！

☑ If only I could fly.
要是我能飛就好了。

☑ I'll be right back.
我馬上回來。

☑ I'll be right there.
我馬上就到。

☑ I'll fix you up.
我會幫你打點的。

☑ I'll just play it by ear.
我到時隨機應變。

☑ I'll see to it.
我會留意的。

☑ I'll see you at six.
我六點鐘見你。

☑ I'm crazy about you.
我為你瘋狂。 / 我為你神魂顛倒。

☑ I'm home.
我回來了。

☑ I'm in a hurry.
我在趕時間。

☑ I'm lost.
　我迷路了。

☑ I'm not sure.
　我不確定。

☑ I'm on a diet.
　我在節食。

☑ I'm on your side.
　我全力支援你。

☑ I'm proud of you.
　我以你為榮。

☑ I'm single.
　我單身。

☑ Incredible!
　不可思議！

☑ Is it true or false?
　這是對的還是錯的？

我是**英語會話王**
I am English Coversation King

☑ Is this yours?
這是你的嗎？

☑ It depends.
看情況。/ 不一定。

☑ It doesn't make sense.
這沒有意義。/ 不合常理。

☑ It hurts.
好痛。

☑ It is growing cool.
天氣漸漸涼爽起來。

☑ It really takes time.
這樣很花時間。

☑ It seems all right.
看來這沒問題。

☑ It sounds great.
聽起來很不錯。

☑ It's up to you.
看你。／ 由你決定。

☑ It's your turn.
輪到你了。

☑ It's a beautiful day.
真是美好的一天。

☑ It's a long story.
說來話長。

☑ It's a pleasure working with you.
與您合作很愉快。

☑ It's against the law.
這是違法的。

☑ It's hard to say.
很難說。

☑ It's no use complaining.
發牢騷沒什麼用。

我是**英語會話王**
I am English Coversation King

☑ It's up to you.
由你決定。

☑ I've been coughing day and night.
我一直在咳嗽。

☑ I've been dying to see you.
我非常想見到你。

☑ I've got a bad cold.
我感冒很嚴重。

☑ I've got a cold.
我感冒了。

☑ I've got a runny nose.
我流鼻涕。

☑ I've got a sore throat.
我喉嚨痛。

☑ I've got a temperature / I'm running a
high fever.

我發燒了。 / 我發高燒。

☑ Just for entertainment.
只是消遣一下。

☑ Keep in touch.
保持聯絡。

☑ Keep it up.
堅持下去。

☑ Kind of.
有點。

☑ Knowledge is power.
知識就是力量。

☑ Leave me alone!
不要打擾我！別管我！

☑ Let bygones be bygones.
過去的，就讓它過去吧。

我是**英語會話王**
I am English Coversation King

☑ Let go.
放手。

☑ Let me see.
讓我想想。

☑ Let's take a rest here.
我們在這邊休息一下吧。

☑ Long time no see.
好久不見。

☑ Make up your mind.
做個決定吧。

☑ Make yourself at home.
別拘束，當作自己家。

☑ May I help you?
我能幫你嗎？

☑ May I use your pen?
我可以用你的筆嗎？

☑ Me, too.
我也是。

☑ My mouth is watering.
我要流口水了。

☑ My pleasure.
我的榮幸。

☑ My treat.
我請客。

☑ Never mind.
不要緊。

☑ Next.
下一位。

☑ Nice to meet you.
我很高興跟你見面。

☑ Nice!
好！

☑ No one knows.
沒有人知道。

☑ No pain no gain.
不勞無獲。

☑ No problem.
沒問題。

☑ No way.
不可能。

☑ No, thank you.
不了，謝謝。

☑ None of your business.
不關你的事。

☑ Nonsense.
胡說。/胡鬧。

☑ Not a sound was heard.
一點聲音也沒有。

Track 122

☑ Not bad.

不錯。

☑ Not exactly.

不全然是這樣。

☑ Not yet.

還沒。

☑ Occupied.

使用中。

☑ Of course.

當然了。

☑ Oh, My God.

噢，天哪。

☑ One more time.

再來一次。

☑ Pardon me?

什麼？／抱歉我沒聽清楚。

☑ Please speak slowly.
請講慢一點。

☑ Please.
請。

☑ Raise your hand.
舉手。

☑ Read it for me.
讀給我聽。

Track 123

☑ Say again.
再說一次。（聽不清楚時）

☑ She has been to Paris.
她有去過巴黎。

☑ She is in Taipei now.
她現在在台北。

☑ She's under the weather.
她心情不好。

☑ Sit down, please.
坐下！

☑ Skating is interesting.
滑冰很有趣。

☑ Slow down.
慢點。

☑ So do I.
我也一樣。

☑ So far so good.
目前還不錯。

☑ Sorry.
對不起。

☑ Speak louder, please.
請說大聲一點。

☑ Stand up, please.
請站起來。

☑ Stop!
停！／站住！

☑ Supper is ready at six.
晚餐六點鐘就好了。

☑ Surprise!
給你一個驚喜！

☑ Take care.
保重。

Track 124

☑ Relax.
放輕鬆。

☑ Take it easy.
別緊張。

☑ Take your time.
慢慢來。

☑ Terrific!
棒極了！

☑ Thank you very much.
非常感謝。

☑ Thank you.
謝謝。

☑ That sounds nice.
聽起來還不錯。

☑ That's going too far.
太離譜了。

☑ That's a good idea.
這個主意真不錯。

☑ That's all I need.
我要的就是這些了。

☑ That's all.
就這樣。

☑ That's always the case.
習以為常了。

☑ That's too much.
太過分了。

☑ That's it.
這樣就對了。

☑ That's right.
沒錯。

☑ That's very nice of you.
你真好。

Track 125

☑ That happens.
常有的事。

☑ The answer is zero.
白忙一場。

☑ The road divides here.
這條路在這裡分岔。

☑ The wall has ears.
隔牆有耳。

☑ This is just what I need.
這正是我所需要的。

☑ This way.
這邊請。

☑ Time's up.
時間到。

☑ Time is money.
時間就是金錢。

☑ Time is running out.
沒時間了。

☑ Time is up.
時間快到了。

☑ Time will tell.
日久見人心。/ 時間會證明一切。

☑ Too expensive.
太貴。

我是英語會話王
I am English Coversation King

☑ Try again.
　再試試。

☑ Unbelievable!
　無法置信！

☑ Wait!
　等一下。

☑ Watch out!
　當心！

Track 126

☑ We are good friends.
　我們是好朋友。

☑ We're all for it.
　我們全都同意。

☑ What a nice day.
　今天天氣真好。

☑ What a pity.
　太遺憾了。

☑ What about you?

你呢？

☑ What date is today?

今天幾月幾號？

☑ What day is today?

今天星期幾？

☑ What do you think?

你認為怎麼樣？

☑ What does he like?

他喜歡什麼？

☑ What happened to you?

你怎麼了？

☑ What is your phone number?

你電話幾號？

☑ What should I do?

我該怎麼辦？。

☑ What time is it?

幾點了？

☑ What's going on?

怎麼了？／ 發生什麼事了？

☑ What's up?

有發生什麼事嗎？／ 最近如何？

☑ What's wrong with you?

你哪裡不對勁？

Track 127

☑ What's your goal in life?

你的人生目標是什麼？

☑ Where is the restroom?

洗手間哪裡？

☑ Which one do you prefer?

你選哪一個？

☑ Who told you so?

誰告訴你的？

Track 127

☑ Who knows?

天知道。

☑ Who is it?

誰？(有人敲門)

☑ Who's calling?

哪一位？（電話中）

☑ Why did you leave your last job?

你為什麼離職呢？

☑ Why not?

好呀！ / 為什麼不呢？

☑ Wonderful!

太棒了！

☑ Would you do me a favor?

可以幫我一個忙嗎？

☑ Would you write it down for me?

可以寫下來給我嗎？

☑ Yes, a little.
會，一點點。

☑ You are just in time.
你來得正是時候。

☑ You are kidding me.
別拿我開玩笑了。

Track 128

☑ You bet!
當然！

☑ You can make it.
你行的。

☑ You chicken.
膽小鬼。

☑ You did a great job.
你做得很好。

☑ You look great!
你看起來棒極了！

☑ You need to workout.
你需要去運動鍛鍊一下。

☑ You owe me one.
你欠我一個人情。

☑ You set me up.
你出賣我。

☑ Your hands feel cold.
你的手摸起來很冷。

☑ You're everything to me.
你是我的一切！

☑ You're welcome.
不客氣。

☑ You've got a point there.
你說得挺有道理的。

☑ What's your name?
你叫什麼名字？

我是**英語會話王**
I am English Coversation King

☑ My name is Ken.
我叫肯。

☑ Where are you from?
你從哪裡來的？

☑ I'm from Canada.
我從加拿大來的。

Track 129

☑ I'm from Taiwan.
我來自台灣。

☑ Where do you live?
你住在哪裡？

☑ I live in England.
我住在英國。

☑ I'm hungry.
我餓了。

☑ Are you hungry?
你會餓嗎？

☑ Are you thirsty?
你會渴嗎？

☑ Would you like to try some?
你要不要吃吃看？

☑ Have you eaten?
你吃過飯了嗎？

☑ What would you like to eat?
你想吃什麼？

☑ I am full.
我飽了。

☑ I have never been to Germany.
我沒有去過德國。

☑ Have you ever been to France?
你有去過法國嗎？

☑ I have been to Canada.
我有去過加拿大。

☑ Is this your first time in Taiwan?
這是你第一次來台灣嗎？

☑ Where is my boarding gate?
我的登機口在哪？

☑ Don't be late.
別遲到。

Track 130

☑ Where is your flight ticket?
你的機票在哪裡？

☑ I prefer a window seat.
我想坐靠窗的位置。

☑ I prefer an aisle seat.
我想坐靠走道的位置。

☑ Take a taxi.
搭計程車。

☑ Please call a taxi for me.
請幫我叫計程車。

Track 130

☑ Please call me a cab.
請幫我叫計程車。

☑ Where can I get a taxi?
我要去哪裡搭計程車？

☑ Where to?
去哪裡？

☑ Please take me to this hotel.
請載我去這間飯店。

☑ Please take me to this address.
請載我到這個地址。

☑ Please take me here.
請載我到這裡。

☑ Please take me to the airport.
請載我到機場。

☑ To this hotel, please.
請到這間飯店。

我是**英語會話王**
I am English Coversation King

☑ Drive slowly.
開慢一點。

☑ Traffic jam.
塞車。

☑ To this address.
到這個地址。

Track 131

☑ To this place.
到這個地方。

☑ To the airport.
到這個機場。

☑ How much is it to Long Beach?
到長灘要多少錢？

☑ Taxi fare.
計程車費。

☑ I want to get off.
我想下車。

Track 131

☑ Let me off.
讓我下車。

☑ Please let me off here.
請讓我在這邊下車。

☑ Please give me the taxi fare receipt.
請給我收據。

☑ Please wait here for a moment.
請在這邊等一下。

☑ Please stop here.
請在這邊停。

☑ How long will you stay in Hong Kong?
你會待在香港多久？

☑ How many days will you stay in Los Angeles?
你會待在洛杉磯幾天？

☑ Help!

我是**英語會話王**
I am English Coversation King

救命！

☑ Run!
快跑！

☑ Go!
走！

☑ Go away!
走開！

Track 132

☑ Get out!
出去！

☑ Watch out!
小心！

☑ Come here.
過來。

☑ Don't move!
不許動！

☑ Don't come close.
不要靠近我。

☑ Stop!
停！

☑ Freeze!
不准動！

☑ On your knees!
跪下！

☑ On your face!
趴下！

☑ Get down!
趴下！

☑ Call the police.
打電話叫警察。

☑ My wallet was stolen.
我錢包被偷了。

☑ My purse was stolen.
我的皮包被偷了。

☑ Thief!
小偷！

☑ Call the police!
叫警察！

☑ My bag was robbed!
我包包被搶了！

☑ Someone is trying to rob me.
有人想要搶劫我的東西。

☑ I was robbed!
我被搶劫了！

☑ Please come quickly!
請趕快來！

☑ I have a stiff neck.
我落枕了。

☑ Somebody got hurt.
有人受傷了。

☑ Please get an ambulance.
請叫救護車。

☑ There is a car accident.
有一起車禍。

☑ There is a fight.
有人在打架。

☑ Fire!
火災！失火了！

☑ Be careful!
小心！

☑ Look out!
當心！

☑ Please help me.
請幫幫我。

☑ Hurry!
赶快！

☑ Are you OK?
你还好吗？

☑ Call the fire brigade!
打电话叫火警！

Track 134

☑ Calm down!
冷静！

☑ Someone broke into my house.
有人闯入我家。

☑ Don't touch me.
不要碰我。

☑ Pervert!
变态！

☑ Somebody intentionally touched my breast!

我被襲胸了！

☑ My child is missing!
我的小孩不見了。

☑ Hands up.
雙手舉起來。

☑ Someone is drowning.
有人溺水了。

☑ She got a heat stroke.
她中暑了。

☑ I can't swim.
我不會游泳。

☑ I got a cramp in my foot.
我腳抽筋了。

☑ I feel dizzy.
我頭好暈。

☑ I feel like I'm about to faint.
我感覺快暈倒了。

☑ Hold on!
撐住啊！

☑ Wait, no.
等等，不行！

Track 135

☑ Cheer up!
振作點！

☑ Let's go.
我們走。

☑ Take it easy.
放輕鬆。

☑ You've got the wrong number.
你打錯了。

☑ I'll call you later.
我晚點打給妳。

☑ Got it.
收到。了解。

☑ Where is the exit?
出口在哪裡？

☑ After you.
你先。